Praise for *Weeping Under This Same Moon...*

"...is a stunning achievement written with uncanny sympathy and intuition from the complementary perspectives of two teenage girls — one a Vietnamese refugee, the other a passionate yet unhappy American high school student — the book vividly portrays very different yet intersecting worlds. It is a moving, heartwarming, even inspiring book. I recommend it enthusiastically to readers of all ages and in particular to young adults."

— George Rupp, President, The International Rescue Committee

"Volunteering can spark an inner joy as Jana Laiz so aptly demonstrates in this compelling and uplifting story. We, at Landmark Volunteers have documented this phenomenon thousands of times: high school volunteers deriving fulfillment and self respect while serving the greater needs of others. I would recommend *Weeping Under This Same Moon* to any adult or young person wishing to see what can happen by the simple act of volunteering."

— Ann B. Barrett, Executive Director Landmark Volunteers

"Another human-and-Earth-friendly book by the author of *Elephants of the Tsunami*! Jana Laiz makes us experience viscerally the plight of refugees everywhere with this tale of Vietnamese Boat People and the American teenager who volunteers to help them make the transition from strangers in a strange land to citizens of a new homeland. Truly a book every young person should read and take a lesson from.

— Isobel Noble, award-winning Author of the ***RUIN*** series.

"With understanding, humor & compassion, Jana Laiz draws us into the interior lives of two teenagers living a world apart. As they share families, stories, languages, customs, food and faiths, these young women come to the place we are all searching for in today's world—'common ground.'"

— Shirley Paukulis, former editor, SAWADDI Magazine (AWC), Bangkok, Thailand

Also by Jana Laiz

Elephants of the Tsunami

The Twelfth Stone
(Coming Soon)

J A N A   L A I Z

WEEPING

UNDER THIS SAME MOON

Crow Flies Press
The Berkshires, Massachusetts

ISBN 0-9814910-0-6

Published by Crow Flies Press

www.crowfliespress.com

To my parents, Joy & Paul Bergins, who let me go so I could find my way back. To P.M.A., the entire Q. family who are still so dear to my heart, and to my little Hoa, now all grown up. You changed my life.

Special thanks to The International Rescue Committee for allowing a seventeen-year-old girl to be a part of history and to make a difference in the world.

They write letters with their blood, to send news home
A lone goose flaps through the clouds
How many families are weeping under this same moon?
The same thought wandering how far apart?

Pity for Prisoners
by Huyen Quang Ly Dao Tai
(1254-1334)

Translated by Burton Raffel

Part I

Mei

Chapter 1

I wait for the man in white to come for us. He will come in the dead of the night when all is still. When the cicadas are singing and the moon is low in the night sky. We have paid for our journey with bars of gold and he will take us to the boat that will be our home until we get to where we will be safe. But I am not sure we will find safety anywhere.

My friend left before me and she was not safe. I want to cry for her, who is lost to me forever. They sent her away and her boat was captured by pirates. I was told how she bravely jumped over the side before they had their brutal way with her. Now she is gone, beneath the China Sea, food for the fish and the sharks. And I will never see her again. Never again will I tell her my secret dreams and desires. Never will I walk with her and drink lemonade. Never will we learn English together like we had planned, nor meet one day in New York

City, the place we dream of going.

My parents will send me, with only my fourteen-year-old brother and tiny sister. My younger sister is too small to carry her own case, so I must carry one for both of us. And so I cannot take my paints or my brushes. I can only take a small case filled with one change of clothing and our toothbrushes.

My parents told me I must sacrifice my pleasures to help them. I tried to explain that my paints and brushes were not for pleasure, but something I needed, perhaps more than I needed clothing or a toothbrush. This made them angry and so I put my paints and my brushes into a large wooden case and buried it in our garden under the wisteria.

If the soldiers loot our house when we are gone, they will not find it. And one day, I will come back for it. One day, when Vietnam is the happy place I remember from when I was as small as my young sister is now.

I lie in my bed, the mosquito net making everything look hazy, and watch as a bat flies past the moon. I will miss this room; my sisters' soft breathing as they sleep, the pictures from the fashion magazines I cut out and paste on the wall next to my small bed. I will miss the smells of my village; the pungent smell of lemon grass and steamed dumplings, cellophane noodle soup simmering with fish freshly caught from the ocean. I will miss longan fruit and star fruit, native to our country. I will miss the cà phê phin, the sweet coffee our country is famous for and I am now finally allowed to drink. I will miss the call of the hawkers as they try to sell their wares. I will miss the temple where I go with my mother every day to pray for our ancestors. I wonder if they will have Buddhist temples where I am going. Mostly I will miss my paints and bamboo brushes made of the finest horsehair. I will miss the scenes of my village that I love to paint (my teacher says so well); the view from our house, the rice paddies, the women in their sarongs and wide brimmed hats to keep the sun from darkening their already tan skin.

But I know we must leave. It is not safe for us anymore. We are of Chinese origin and we are not welcomed here any longer, even though we have called Vietnam our home for many generations. The war is over, but all that remains of our life is this house, which they will soon take from us. My father's once thriving business is now worthless and our wealth is gone. We have only the hidden gold bars for our journey to the west. How ironic. They want us to leave yet they make us pay to do so.

And so I wait for the man in white, each day anticipating his arrival, and each night relieved that he hasn't come. But he will come soon, I know, and I must be ready to go when he does.

Chapter 2

I feel as though I should spend every moment with my mother and father, sisters and brothers. I might never see them again. Our fate may be like that of my dear friend, Vinh. Or like that of my auntie, whose boat ran out of water and who was so thirsty that she drank seawater and died.

But I try not to think this way. What would I do, just sit and cry as I look at their faces, faces that might become faded memories? So I spend my time walking through my village, memorizing the sights and smells and sounds. Usually my little sister, the one who is to go with me, tags along behind me. I try to shoo her away, but she has become very attached to me. She barely speaks to our mother anymore. Is she angry because she knows they will be sending her away first? Doesn't she realize that our parents are doing this for her own protection and safety? This is what I must tell myself, but I suppose if I were her age and being sent far away to an unknown land, I might be angry too.

So she clings to me as though I were her mother. I understand I will have to take on that role. I wonder for how long.

We are acting strangely, all of us. As if nothing is wrong, as if everything is wrong. We don't know how to act. Normal would feel false, yet we can't behave as if one of us has died. We are all still alive and well. Just waiting for when the man in white comes for us, one little group at a time.

And so we are stuck. Smiling too brightly, talking too loudly, cleaning too vigorously. My mother tries to cook her most delicious dishes with the meager rations we have. She makes us eat together, dinner at least, all thirteen of us, at the big teak table that no longer glistens. Polishing it has lost its importance, though it still feels smooth when I run my fingers along the dark wood. And we try to have pleasant conversation and talk of small things. Of old neighbor Trinh's runaway pig, of the new statue of Ho Chi Minh in the square. But every bite of food is laced with fear and sadness. The rice lies heavy in the stomach and there is bitterness to every bite that can't be washed away even by the sweetest coffee. I have tried to paint my family, to have a portrait of remembrance to take on my long journey, but every time I try, the colors bleed, the brush strokes are rough, the rice paper rips.

I ask my mother for an old photograph. There is only one with all of us and she won't let me have it. Instead, she gives me one of seven of my brothers and sisters at the beach, playing on the sand. It is in color and it is a happy picture of happier times. I place it carefully into my case. In my case I find a letter in my mother's hand. I do not read it. It was not meant for now. I will wait until I am gone from here, when I can cry freely without causing my mother more grief than she already feels.

I had heard of parents sending their children away during wartime for their own safety. I never understood a mother who could do that. I never thought my mother could. Wouldn't she rather us all die together than be separated? Doesn't she love us enough to keep us together even though we might be in danger? How can she let us go? But I know what the answer is. Of course she loves us, which is why she is giving us this chance. And her hope is that one by one, we will find each other in our new home and be together again. Start over again.

If we stay, life will become unbearable. We cannot stay and expect to live the same kind of life we once had. The Vietnamese don't want us here. The new communist government wants to rid Vietnam of all Chinese, which means my family. My father was a rich merchant, but his wealth is gone along with his pride. He looks broken somehow, sad and defeated. He was proud of being Vietnamese. Being Chinese came second. But they will put us in concentration camps if we stay. I wonder if he feels like the Jews must have felt during their terrible time in Germany. I do. I wonder that times have not changed from 1940 to 1976. Part of me is glad to go. Why would I want to stay in a place where I am hated? And yet I don't believe my neighbors hate me. Everyone is just confused. The war affected too many of us.

I wonder what my new home will be like. Will I make friends quickly or will I be an outcast, a stranger? Will we be sent to America, Australia, Canada, France? I hear all the wonderful things about America, and I hope it is the place we are to go, but I am not so gullible as some, so I withhold judgment. I will wait until I get there, if I get there.

Chapter 3

We cannot find my third sister. No one has seen her for several hours and this is unusual, for she is always at my fifth sister's side. They are only two years apart with a brother between them and practically inseparable. My mother is getting worried as the sun sets and still no sign of her. I have looked in all her familiar spots; the cool back veranda, high in the acacia tree, behind the rock in the garden.

My fifth sister looks everywhere she can think of, and she knows more places than I, for they tell each other everything and go everywhere together. I cannot imagine where she has gone and frightening thoughts that I do not want to give voice to are entering my mind. I feel we are all thinking similar thoughts though no one dares speak of them.

I put on the rice for our supper and go into the room we share. Perhaps she has returned. But the room is empty, the white mosquito nets shifting in the slight breeze. I sit on my bed, trying to become my third sister, trying to enter her mind and find out where she is hiding, or, I think with a shiver, where she was taken. I concentrate hard, letting myself imagine I am looking through her eyes, but my thoughts are mingled with fear and so it does not work. We have played this game before, trying to get a glimpse into each other's minds and emotions. We are more often than not correct. Sometimes it frightens us, this strange accuracy we share. But it is not a game I am playing now. I am frightened and I want my sister home with me.

Suddenly, I feel a light touch on my leg. I gasp and then quickly brush it off, thinking it must be a spider or a lizard bold enough to come too close. I look down at the floor and see a hand dart out from under the bed and touch me again. I am flooded with relief when I realize that it is my sister, hiding there. Has she been here all day?

I bend down and very quietly look under the bed. There is not even a speck of dust, only my sister curled up like a baby with a pillow and a sheet. She looks frightened and I ask her what she is doing hiding under my bed for such a long time. She whispers for me to join her, so I do. She hugs me to her and I put my arms around her, stroke her hair.

"I am frightened," she tells me. "Frightened of the man in white. He is a ghost who will take me to my grave. That is where you will go when he comes for you, so you must not go. Stay here with me."

I try to reassure her that this is not so, but my voice does not sound as steady as I intend it to. I am not convincing her or myself.

We stay this way for some time, until I remember that I must inform our mother she is safe. She begs me not to give her away, but I tell her that mother is sick with worry and that will do no one any good. She lets me bring her forth from her hiding place and puts her head down when my parents scold her for causing such distress.

Late at night I see her sitting near my mother, who is stroking her hair and speaking words of comfort. The words touch me, but I will be the first to leave, so they offer me little reassurance. I go to my bed and think for a moment about getting my pillow and blanket and hiding myself as well. But that will solve nothing. I close my eyes and fall asleep to the soft sounds of my mother's words drifting on the breeze. Perhaps they comfort me more than I realize.

Chapter 4

The man in white has come for us. I was sleeping when he came, but my father was awake, like he is every night, waiting for the man whom he hopes will take his children away to safety and not to death or drowning on the open sea. He wakes me gently, rocking my shoulder. In a gesture very uncharacteristic, he puts his head next to mine and begins to cry. I cry too, gripping him, my knuckles white against his dark robe. I have never been away from my family before and I am consumed with fear. My father is shaking as we cry together. But the man in white is waiting and I must leave.

My two sisters with whom I share this room have awakened and they are staring wide-eyed at the scene playing out before them. They throw themselves upon one another and begin to sob.

My father abruptly stops his tears. Wipes his eyes briskly

with his shirtsleeve. He places his hands on my shoulders, his eyes penetrating mine. His look is filled with such deep sadness that I cannot breathe. I gasp for air in between sobs. He holds me close for a moment and I do not want to let him go. He separates us and kisses my cheek, my tears mingling with his own.

"My best child, my number one, I am loathe to let you go, but we have talked of this before. I will pray to Kuan Yin every day for your safety and for our reunion. Take care of your little sister and brother. I have faith in you, my artist, my flower."

My father moves from me, touching each of my sisters gently as he goes out to wake the other two and I go into my mother's bedroom where she, too, has awakened. She looks at me, eyes wide with fear, knowing why I am in her room at this time of night. She begins to wail, tears streaming down her aging face, waking the household. I grab hold of her, trying to calm her, yet I am as desperate as she. More so. But she is consumed with guilt and rage at those who are forcing this to happen. She gulps for breath and her grief adds to mine. We grip each other with force, wailing, screaming, begging the man in white to go away, for the time to be some other. I hear crying from all over the house. We should be still, but how can anyone keep silent in the midst of such misery?

My father, case in hand, pulls me off her. She reaches, grasping the air for me, clutching at what she cannot have, stricken with grief that she may never see me again. My sisters and brothers are all crying, some pounding the floor, some holding on to each other for support. My little sister grabs my leg and hides behind me. My brother takes my father's hand. He has not done this in a long time. He is fourteen and full of bravado, but right now he looks small and vulnerable. I see how this gesture touches my father, who is overwhelmed with despair.

I cannot say goodbye, so I say nothing. I give them all a last look, filled with meaning, filled with uncertainty, filled with anguish, and follow my father out into the night.

Chapter 5

The boat is small but packed tightly with sorrowful looking people. My brother tries to count their miserable faces, but loses count after seventy-five. My father could only walk us as far as the entrance to the path leading to the water. We stood for a very long time, embracing in the hot night, huddled together, staring at one another so as not to forget. My father lifted my sister into his arms, holding her close. Impatiently, the man in white drew us from him and forbade him to follow. I turned once as we made our way down the path toward the boat. My father had fallen to his knees, his head in his hands. My sister tried to turn, but I steered her straight ahead, my hands gripping her perhaps too tightly. I cannot erase that image from my mind and am glad she will not have to add it to her memories. When I saw the boat I was glad my father was not able to see us off. He would never have forgiven himself for allowing us to embark upon this journey in a boat too small for fifty people.

The vessel is old and wooden, with a small area at one end that has some cover against the weather. Just a canvas tent-like cover where the majority of people are huddled. I can see there will be no room for us under that small bit of shelter. I wonder how we will eat, where the water is, if there will be enough, but I keep silent. I am afraid to know.

We push our way into the middle as my mother instructed. "It is safer there," she had said. I was unsure how she knew this. If pirates come or a typhoon blows will we not all be in danger?

People grapple for space and we are shoved and cramped and practically on top of one another as the boat leaves the dock. The driver tells us harshly to be quiet, that we will be caught if we make any more noise. Finally everyone settles down as we drift out of the harbor, the engines off, the only sound that of the driver dipping his paddle into the sea.

When we enter open water, the engines are turned on and we sit like statues, anticipating the worst, but all remains quiet. It is still dark, but there is a faint glow on the horizon. If it were another time, I might think it beautiful, worthy of painting, the sky turning from deep blue to steel gray, to pink. The stars melting into their place above us, remaining in their position, though unseen.

My sister, Linh, is green-looking. She doesn't want to eat the sticky rice that my mother wrapped for us in banana leaves. She clings to me, calling me "mother," her face bathed in cold sweat. I snap at her and tell her to stop.

"I am not your mother!" But she refuses to stop and so I

let her. If it helps her, who am I to argue?

I try to imagine a scene in which I am meeting my family again, in a safe place. Where I will be able to teach them all I know of our new home. I will be the first to arrive there, so I will be the one who will know where the shops are, where to buy vegetables, where to wash the clothes. My father and mother will be the last to leave, sending all the others ahead of them except for the two baby girls. I was glad not to have the responsibility for those two. Linh is young enough and already I am assuming the role of mother.

At sea, the third day, I pull out the letter from my mother. I hold it in my hand for a long time before I have the courage to open it. I couldn't bring myself to read it sooner. I read it under a blanket, during the bright day, so that I can let only enough light in to see her words, but dark enough so that I can pretend I am alone. I let her words enter my mind slowly and deliberately, trying to hear her voice aloud in my head as I read it. Linh tugs at the blanket, but I ignore her long enough to allow myself to cry for some time. I hug the letter to my breast; gripping it so hard I crumple it. Here is what it says:

My oldest daughter,

As I write this letter I imagine you sitting on a small boat somewhere in the middle of the China Sea. I pray you are safe and far from harm, neither hungry nor thirsty. I am wretched and heartbroken that I have to send you away and I am oh so angry at Vietnam, at the communists, at Kuan Yin, at Buddha himself, for putting us all in this terrible position. Maybe it is our karma for being Chinese, the Jews of Asia, so we have been called. Please forgive me for sending you from your family and all you hold dear. Forgive me for not letting you take your brushes and paints. I promise I will buy you a new set when we are together again. There will be much to paint in our new home, I am sure.

There is so much I want to tell you, so much I want to say, but the words are lodged deep in my throat and they make me choke with sorrow and tears. Please forgive me for putting such a terrible burden on you. Remember, you are the eldest and must take care of your younger brother and sister in my stead. I am so sorry that you must be expected to play the role of mother to them. Yet that is what I am asking you to do! What you must do! And I am confident that you will do a fine job looking after them. Please send them to school and take them to a temple where I hope you will carry on our traditions. Don't forget that Tuan loves mung bean cakes and little Linh gets cold easily. And you, my number one daughter, you love to paint and I have taken that from you. I am so sorry. Find some paints when you are someplace safe.

Oh, I cannot see what I write, so full of tears are these old eyes!

Forgive me! I wish I could change things as they are, but I cannot. I only hope you will one day forgive me for sending you away. My stomach tightens as I write this and you are sitting in the next room, playing with your sisters.

And so I can only tell you how much you mean to me, how much I love and cherish you. You, my first born child, my artist, my flower. Think of me with love and tenderness. And forgiveness.

I do not know when we will see each other again, but I will see you every night when I lie down to sleep and I will instruct my soul to find you in my dreams.

Look for me.

Your loving mother.

I can only read it when I can hide under my blanket, for it makes my insides ache and the tears come. And so I look every night for my mother to come to me in my dreams. And sometimes I remember seeing her. And I think of her all the time.

People sit, weeping quietly, shaking their heads in anguish, likely remembering those left behind or fearful of their unknown futures. Many are sick, leaning over the side of the boat, their bile mixing in the rough water.

There are some boys a bit younger than my brother. They occupy their time wrestling with their thumbs. My brother does not join them; he is too busy being conscientious, looking after me and my sister. I am glad he is behaving so grown up, but I would not mind if he played with those other boys every once in a while.

I hope we can all remain friendly. I have heard stories of too many days on board with too much time and not enough food or water. The stories are not pleasant. So I keep to myself, merely nodding and smiling at those near me. I will not get close to anyone, nor let anyone know me. I must be responsible for myself, my brother and sister. I must concentrate on our safety with no distractions. There is a young man who looks in my direction every now and then, but I put my eyes down whenever I catch a glimpse of him looking. Now is not the time for new friendships, or so I tell myself.

Chapter 6

The first days on the boat are the worst. I thought I would be immune to the sickness, but I am not and spend many hours leaning over the side of the boat, heaving what small remains of rice and broth lay in my stomach. My pants are getting bigger and bigger and I have to hold them up with the one safety pin I was smart enough to bring. My little sister cries from hunger and yet she cannot eat more than a few bites. I force her to drink the little amounts of water they ration to us. She cries when I force her, but I do not care. I will force this, if I cannot force her to eat.

The food is bad. Sometimes the rice moves and I think I am imagining it. I know that rice cannot move. No, mixed with the rice are maggots. They blend perfectly in size and color with the smooth whiteness of the rice. I pretend not to notice, but perhaps they are the cause of my stomach distress.

Those people who are not too weak are beginning to bicker and quarrel. Someone did not clean up after themselves when going to the toilet, which is actually a bucket that is poured over the side and dipped into the water and rinsed. The smell is horrendous and makes me gag every time I need to relieve myself. Another person has taken an inch more space than is acceptable. Someone is looking at another's daughter in a strange and suspicious way. I am weary of it.

The one time I spoke up and said we should thank Kuan Yin that we have not been visited by pirates, everyone gasped and made signs against evil. I keep to myself now and tell my brother and sister to do the same.

And then there is the old woman who talks and shrieks to herself incessantly. "Don't go out into the paddies, don't go out there!" She repeats over and over, day and night, until we all want to scream. The boatman yells for her to shut her mouth. How can he be so unkind, and yet I feel the same way. I want her to stop! She makes me afraid and unable to sleep. Even after she finally falls into a troubled, fitful sleep, I stay awake wondering what happened to her. My heart goes out to her. She must have lost those dear to her and now she is demented. No one even tries to comfort her, for she looks at us with unseeing eyes. I wonder who put her on this boat; she is obviously alone, but I have to care for my siblings and cannot leave my sister alone to try and calm this old woman.

My brother, Tuan, is one of the only ones who has not had to give his food up to the sea. He is strong and hearty, for which I am grateful. Sometimes, before it is time for sleep, Tuan pulls his thin blanket near to me and my sister. He props himself up on one elbow, his hand cupping his thin face and tells us funny stories that he makes up in his head. He talks quietly. These stories are just for us. They are about many things. Flying dragons, talking monkeys, demon lovers reuniting, ghost warriors saving ladies in distress. The stories keep my sister up for more hours than necessary, but they give her mind something pleasant to seize upon. They are a diversion from the steady boredom and fear that pervades us.

I pray to Kuan Yin every night as I lie on my rough blanket, looking up at the stars, my baby sister curled at my side like a cat. I know my mother and father are praying to her as well, and I imagine we are praying together and she is hearing one voice, asking for protection and reunion. I pray quietly. My sister sleeps the sleep of a child, but when her eyes are open, I see they have become bigger in her small face, and there are dark circles around them.

I hope we are getting close to land, but all I see when I stand up to stretch my aching, cramped legs, is water and more water.

We saw a whale, off in the distance. Many people screamed, imagining the creature would cause our small vessel to capsize. I knew it was not close enough to do us any harm. I smiled at the beauty and freedom of the beast, wishing I were free to swim and play as she. I imagined jumping overboard and catching hold of her smooth body, allowing myself to be pulled along, faster and faster until I too disappeared beneath the dark, silky surface.

Chapter 7

When are we going to arrive? The sea stretches on endlessly, the time, interminably. There is only the steady rocking and creaking of the vessel. One of the boys Tuan's age has taken it upon himself to record our days here. Every morning he takes his pen from his pocket and puts a line on the side of the boat. It is easy to lose count of the days and so far I count eight marks. I have heard of boats on the sea for weeks. The men occupy their time smoking what cigarettes they ration themselves. Women cry, babies wail constantly. The old lady has quieted down, and now she sits on her hands and rocks.

Fresh water is getting scarcer and scarcer. People have begun to hoard what they can, getting suspicious of everyone's greetings, gestures, small talk, thinking there is some hidden motive. Are you trying to ingratiate yourself to get an extra ration of my rice or a thimbleful of my water? It feels uncomfortable and strange. Our camaraderie has become laced with mistrust. We are only trying to survive, but now I see that everyone is out for themselves and I must be too. I have a brother and sister to care for.

My stomach is concave now. My cheap wristwatch hangs off my wrist. I don't know why I bother to wear it. It stopped working days ago. Looking at it gives me comfort. I bought it one day with my mother and second sister. We were walking the busy streets of Saigon, now known as Ho Chi Minh City, and a hawker was selling small watches on the street. My mother normally would never stop for such as he, but his eyes seemed kind and the watches he displayed looked elegant, even to my mother. We stopped and looked. One of a kind, he told her. My mother chose one for each of us. Just the three of us. She bargained so hard, I felt ashamed. He would never make any money on this sale, but he agreed with my mother's final offer and handed each of us our watches after she handed him the money. He had seen my embarrassment and winked at me when my mother turned to leave. I smiled and he laughed out loud, pulling identical watches out of his jacket, putting them back onto his small display box.

I will try to replace the battery when I am somewhere in the world that is civilized. Where people are not hiding bits of rice wrapped in handkerchiefs under their shirts. I wonder when that time will be.

I see the sky in the distance turning dark, covering the sun. Low clouds fill with rain. For a brief moment, my artist's mind finds it beautiful and I itch to paint the scene, but no, what it tells me is that a storm is coming and this is what I fear the most. The swells and rushing of the sea. The boat lifting and lurching to either side. The vomit and stench of seasickness. When the sea is calm, people throw up over the side, but a storm will make them lose all dignity and they will puke where they lie. The smell makes me heave if the swaying and rocking of the sea doesn't. And the cold and salty water spraying, cloying, makes everything damp and sticky.

I want a bath with hot water and soap. My hair feels like wet straw. Though it has not been so long on this boat, it feels like my hair has grown inches and is hard to manage. I know I smell bad, because the smell of bodily odors are all around me and I am sure that I am no exception. I am glad there is no mirror. The young man with the kind eyes has stopped looking in my direction. I almost wish he hadn't. At least when he was looking I felt alive, as though I might still be pretty. Now I feel ugly. And clammy. All the time.

I watch the sky change color and darken, see the swells rising. The boatman tries to steady the craft, but the storm is coming toward us and there is no place to find shelter.

It hits with such force I think we might be swallowed up by the salty waves. Lightning illuminates the sky and thunder cracks like bullets over our heads. People are screaming. My brother, sister and I huddle under our rough blankets, shivering from fear, trying to keep our stomachs from heaving what little is inside. Those lucky enough to be under the small covering group together as if they are old friends. Water sloshes over the sides of the boat and we feel chilled as the cold water splashes and sprays over us, through our thin cover. People hold on to one another, objects slide on water mixed with slime, as we lurch with the swells. And then the sky opens and rain comes pouring down in torrents, the heavens dropping buckets of water down on our heads.

And suddenly, as if this isn't bad enough, the old shrieking woman gets up, makes her way to the side of the boat, and climbs onto the edge. We watch her as if we are watching a play, no one moves to stop her, no one really believing she will do what she obviously is about to do. It is happening so fast; a wave hits the boat hard and when we look again, she is gone. People are shouting to the boatman, and those brave enough to leave their imagined safety, grip the side of the boat to look for her, ready to throw a rope or a float to her, but she is gone beneath the roiling waves.

The storm rages on but we are in shock, not knowing whether we have just enabled her suicide or watched an accident occur. I can hear weeping over the wind and rain and wonder if it is my fellow passengers or if it is the old woman weeping beneath the waves. I think there will be no peace for her; the sea is not a quiet place today.

Chapter 8

We saw land today. It was far off in the distance, but it was solid and green. My heart leapt when I saw it, but it also seized with fear. We have been on this vessel for so long, it has become uncomfortably familiar. The thought of leaving it is exhilarating and terrifying at the same time. Leaving behind the stench of seasickness, the wormy rice, the brackish water; this sounds wonderful. But for what? What will our life be like off the boat? What kind nation will let us onto its shores? Will they take care of us while we wait to find a new home? I count the marks again today and count eleven.

We are all tired and ailing, so very hungry and thirsty and extremely bad tempered. I have muscle cramps from lack of movement and my neck constantly aches from sleeping on my elbow. I do not know if I will ever be clean again. Even my strong brother looks scrawny and terribly filthy. Thank Kuan

Yin, he still has his humor.

Tonight Tuan has no stories. His face is serious as he tells us that when we reach land, no matter what, we will stick together. He says that he will always take care of us, and even though I am some years older than he, this brings me comfort. Little Linh has become nothing more than a wisp of a thing. Her thin and faded flowered dress hangs off her and she looks like a rag doll. I try to pull a brush through her hair, but it has become sticky and matted and she cries when I try. If our mother could see us now, she would not recognize us, I am sure.

A cricket was on our boat today. No one knows how it came to be there, but there it was. A brilliant green cricket. Did it jump off a whale's back and onto our boat? Or was it hiding from the start and happened to emerge today? Not that it matters anymore. The superstitious old men and women became frantic, shouting about good omens and trying to catch the poor thing. One old man grabbed his case and pulled out a tiny cricket cage made of bamboo and palm fronds. He and the others were pushing and shoving to try and catch it. When one finally did, others began grabbing for it and the poor cricket was crushed in the fray. It became very quiet; everyone staring at the dead cricket in the old man's withered hand. Now they speak in low tones, one blaming the other. Bad omen. Bad luck.

A woman took the cricket out of the old man's hand and threw it overboard. We watched as its bright green body bobbed on the waves until it became a mere speck.

I hear whispers that we will land very soon. My heart beats erratically in my throat as I think about what will become of us. We will try Malaysia first, and if they say no and tell us to leave, we will try for Hong Kong. We are Chinese after all. They should be required to accept us.

I have heard stories about the camps and it is for this reason I am afraid to leave the security of our little ship, unpleasant though it may be. I am afraid of mosquitoes that carry malaria. I have heard of the shakes and fevers those tiny bugs inflict. When I was a child I contracted a mosquito-born illness such as I never want to experience again. My head felt stabbed with a thousand knives and then sawed over and over again. My stomach contents left me and when everything from it was gone, I retched air and bile, until it felt as though I would heave my own heart.

I fear mosquitoes and what their bites can do. And I fear rats, the size of housecats. I hope this description is merely the exaggerations of those trying to sound thrilling.

I have heard in hushed tones what some guards do to girls and women. And what girls my age have done to get some meat or fish for their bowls. I would rather eat moldy rice than do what they have done. I will put a knife to my throat before I allow myself to trade my soul for a piece of fish.

I am counting on my brother and my wits to keep us safe. I will never let Linh out of my sight. I will stay near the older couple who travel with us. I will fight if I have to. I will fight and I will study English with my tattered old book. Perhaps I will find a teacher. Who knows if they will send us to an English speaking country like we hope, but maybe if I can communicate, they will send us to America, and soon.

It is my turn to cook the evening meal. We are now taking turns, those of us who have the skill. There was practically a mutiny launched on the cook. He cares nothing for taste and after many days, we grew angry and tired of his flavorless rice and broth. We have grown used to the maggots, but we must have something to satisfy our taste buds. There are a few spices left and one bottle of fish sauce, which we use sparingly.

The water is calm tonight and several young men are trying to catch fish for us. My brother holds a line in the water. It relieves boredom if nothing else. But I hope they catch something. My mother taught me to cook and I am a capable one. I light the small stove that has barely anymore propane and begin to make the broth. How I would love some fish to add to the bland soup I will prepare.

Chapter 9

Everyone is yelling about bad omens; the death of the cricket, the death of the old woman. Are we lost at sea? I no longer have a sense of direction. We thought that land was near, but maybe it was only a mirage we saw the other day. I remember the cricket and know it was no mirage. We saw land, but it is not where we are to go. How much longer must we suffer on this floating prison? I am growing bad tempered and anxious. Sometimes I have trouble breathing. My breath comes in short bursts and my heart beats too quickly.

It is hot today, hotter than it has been in days and I long to strip and dive into the cool blue water of the China Sea.

I love to swim. My family went to the shore many times when I was a small child. That was before the war. Before the Americans arrived. Before the communists took over. It has been a long time since we went to the beach for a holiday.

There have been no holidays for many years.

We were a rich family once. We had two houses, one in Saigon and the other in the countryside. The government seized the house in Ho Chi Minh City, and the one we live in now, or the one my family still occupies, I should say, is going to be seized soon. They were both furnished beautifully, with teak wood tables and chairs, and mother-of-pearl inlaid in the glass windows. Someone threw rocks at our beautiful windows and now they are covered with cardboard and tape.

Sometimes when the nights seem to go on forever and I am keeping watch over my little sister, I like to close my eyes and take a walk through my house. I see it as it was. The wood glistening to a shine, the bowl on the table filled with colorful and tasty fruit. I see my mother in the kitchen with our cook, Nguyet, preparing Cat Sot Ca, my favorite fish dish. My visions are sometimes so real that I can smell the whitefish simmering in its tomato broth.

I see my sisters and brothers sitting on the burnished wood floors, playing caps or marbles. I hear my mother scolding them to stop; they will scratch the wood.

I see myself sprawled in my room, my paints and brushes in their water bowls, laid out on the floor. The roll of rice paper spread long, held down on either side with rocks I collected from the river near our summer home. I see myself dipping my brush into the paints and touching it to the paper. The colors turn into sunsets, flowers, a bird in a tree. I refuse to let this paper rip or these colors bleed. No, these are perfect, like my memories. No flaws, no troubles, no war. Just happy times and vivid colors.

I open my eyes and see the stars. They are very bright and

fill the sky. Sometimes there are so many that it scares me. I feel I could be swallowed up by them. When the moon is reflected in the dark ocean, that frightens me too. Swallowed up or swallowed down. My only safety, this small vessel, separating one from the other.

Other times they give me comfort. I imagine myself as part of the whole universe and I do not feel so small after all. Even a shattered star can shine brightly and be seen long after it has died.

Chapter 10

The boat landed in the middle of the night. We all woke to bright, harsh lights shining on us and loud words, severely spoken in a language we do not understand. I think we are in Malaysia and I think we are not welcome. We have heard stories of Malaysian officials shooting refugees or sending them back to sea. I do not understand why we have come to a place where we will not be accepted. Why did we not go to Hong Kong? Hong Kong seemed to me to be in the right direction when my father showed me on his ancient map; away from Vietnam, and closer to the west. And full of Chinese. Maybe our ancestors, relatives.

If they send us away, I do not think I will be able to endure it. If we must stay on this floating devil for another three weeks or however long we have been at sea (I have lost all track of time) I am afraid my little sister will die. She is wasting away. She cries in her sleep, I think from hunger. I hardly ever sleep anymore, spending my nights watching her breathe; to make sure she lives until the next day. She seems to have forgotten my name and constantly calls me 'mother,' even in her sleep. The people on board think I have a child and no husband and they look at me strangely. I am past caring.

I am so very tired. I would like to get out of this boat and walk on solid ground, if only for a moment. And then I want to lie down on a bed made of quilts, with a soft pillow under my neck. My scratchy woolen blanket is full of lice and though I have tried to keep clean, I think I might need to shave off my hair once we have landed. I would like to burn everything I have brought with me in my little case. My sister's clothes and mine. I want us each to have a new dress and new shoes, some hair bows and clean underwear. I do not know if my brother thinks about these things. He is busy trying to be brave.

We are all watching to see what the camp authorities will do with us. We talk in hushed whispers, those of us that still talk to one another. Many on the boat remain silent as they have been these many days. But I know what they are thinking. Will they send us back to sea? Will they make room for us? I am almost too tired to care. I dreamed of landing on friendly shores to smiling faced camp workers, laden with bowls of hot sticky rice, simmering broth and fresh vegetables. Arms filled with clean towels and bars of soap, leading us to steaming hot showers where we had no time limit and everyone went first.

But are dreams ever what one really expects? The camp

officer is screaming at our boatman, waving his arms, flailing, his eyes bulging from his head. People near me start to shout loudly. "How much more can we endure?" they cry. "Take us! Take us!" One woman holds her arms out toward the camp officer. He doesn't see the pathetic gesture, or if he does, ignores it. My sister is still asleep and this frightens me. With all the hubbub shouldn't she be awake? I lean down to listen and I am relieved to hear her soft breathing. I hope her dreams are lovely and that she can stay asleep until we are back out to sea, or being led to our beds.

Chapter 11

We are to stay. I am so relieved I feel like weeping. We are not allowed to get off the boat until the camp doctor has assessed our health, and that means a few more days on this boat. I can endure this now that I know it is for a measured time. A day or two, but not weeks or months. And they will bring us fresh supplies of food. And water. Hopefully clean and perhaps even cold water.

One by one, the doctor will examine us, making sure we are not carrying tuberculosis, malaria, yellow fever, hepatitis, lice. I am sure he will find that we all are sheltering those tiny despicable creatures in our blankets and on our bodies. Will they shave us all or sprinkle foul powder over us?

Everyone is opening his case, checking her belongings. Making sure all their possessions are accounted for. No one seems to have anything worth stealing, but nevertheless, what little each took must be important. Making the choice of what to bring, those lucky enough to have had a choice, must have been very difficult. Entire lives lived in homes filled with possessions, cherished items, wedding gifts, photographs, baby teeth; all the things that make up a life, to be stuffed into one small case! My, how to choose! If I had had a choice, I of course, would have brought my paints and brushes, my beautiful dress that my mother bought for my 16th birthday. I would have taken my gold bangles and my jade earrings. But those were sold to buy food after we lost everything. I would have taken the china elephant my grand-uncle brought me from a trip to India. I might have brought my fancy straw hat.

But I was not given a choice. Everything I love is left behind. And so in my case there are only several changes of undergarments and clothing for my sister and myself, my boar bristle hair brush, our toothbrushes and tooth powder, a roll of toilet paper, a tattered English phrase book, our identity papers, the photo of some of us at the beach and the letter from my mother. That, I have smoothed and read fifty times over.

I am hoping to be able to call her once we are settled, if there is a telephone in the camp. We still had a telephone when I left. I am hopeful that we still do. Although, I am afraid of how I might behave when I hear her voice. Babyish and tearful. Because right now, I want to be cared for, looked after. Like when I was a child and I was sick and my mother would bathe my forehead with cool damp cloths and sing me songs. And rub my back.

But I am not a child any longer. I am a young woman, with two siblings to care for. I must be strong and not allow weakness or despair to engulf me. I look through my case and I see that all our belongings are in order. I take out the old English book and open randomly to a page.

"At what time do you take the evening meal?"

"At what hour do you arise in the morning?"

I repeat the phrases and hope they will come in useful when we get to America or wherever we are to live in the world. I don't even know if I am pronouncing the words correctly.

Enough.

I put the book back into my case. I realize that I am still gripping my mother's letter and I put the crumpled, beloved note into a small, satin-lined, secret pocket on the side of the case and snap it shut. I must be ready for whatever comes next.

Chapter 12

The official Malaysian doctor has found us to be in acceptable health. One by one we were taken to a cordoned off area of the boat, with moveable screens for privacy. He looked in our mouths and in our ears and he examined areas I would rather not have allowed this stranger to see. I demanded to stay with my sister for her examination.

We all carry small intruders on our bodies that must be removed. I am hoping we are not poisoned in the process, but I long to be rid of them and alone with myself again.

My frail, little sister has begun to eat now that we are docked and the rocking of the craft is minimal. There is a little color back in her cheeks, for which I am thankful. With what coins we have hidden, we have bribed the guards to bring us fresh food and the spices they use here, which are not what we are used to, but flavorful, nonetheless. There is an abundance of coconut milk. We do not normally use it, but that is of little consequence. We will use it because it is available and we are hungry. How strange that our countries are so close in proximity, yet worlds apart in cuisine.

My brother is ready to jump overboard to set his feet on dry land again, but I tell him to be patient. Soon enough we will be brought to our new temporary home. And soon enough we will be itching to leave there to continue this arduous journey to our final destination.

I look forward to washing our clothes by the banks of the stream I hear is near the camp. I wonder if there will be an English class. I know some, like us, hope to be destined for America or Canada or Australia, though many want to continue on to France, where they have relatives waiting for them.

I want my mother and father to know we are safely landed on Malaysia's shores. They must be beside themselves with worry. I wonder if the man in white has come for the next group of my siblings. I hope they are safe wherever they are. How dreadful, this not knowing.

"Mother," my sister calls, "When can we leave? I want to pick those flowers!" She points to the shore where brightly colored wildflowers line the beach. I smile for the first time in weeks, and it feels good and strange. She smiles back, her gaunt face lit with childlike joy. She quietly takes my hand and I feel a surge of love toward her. If I must be a mother, she is a good daughter. But I want to be her sister and I hope that one day soon, we will call our own true mother, 'Mother.'

Chapter 13

The camp is so dirty. And so crowded. We walked to it on wobbly legs, as if we were drunkards. I can still feel the sway of the ocean, the steady rocking of the sea. Lines of staggering people following the guards to their new homes. If we weren't so tired and miserable it might have seemed comical. My brother frowned and my sister whimpered when they saw our lodgings. I felt nothing, perhaps because I held no expectations. It is a tiny hut, perhaps two square meters, with one long raised frame with bamboo slats that serve as a bed. Each space has a woven mat and a crude cloth for a blanket. I am glad we do not have to lie on the dirt floor. I am very much afraid of rats.

We are not the only ones in this hut. We share it with a family of eight. They will have to make room for us on this long bed. The mother did not look pleased to see us, but one of the children smiled, faintly. There was no hot rice or simmering broth, no steaming showers or clean towels. Just this tiny, dirty hut. There are grubby, runny-nosed children playing with bottle caps on the grimy floor. Linh is looking at them curiously. Although I would like to keep her as clean as possible, I will not discourage her if she wants to join them in play. I would like to lie down on my space on the bed and fall into a long, dreamless sleep, but I cannot. I must take the tour with the guard as he shows us where we will use the toilet, where to brush our teeth, where to cook and from whom to buy food. We are not allowed out of the camp, although there is a village nearby, with an open market. Someone actually questioned the authority of the guard about this. His cold response was only, "You are forbidden to leave the confines of the camp."

My parents gave me money for food, but for nothing else. I have it hidden so tightly, I have almost forgotten where it is. I will have to bargain hard for everything. It is not my favorite thing to do. It does not come naturally to me as it does to my mother. She is the hardest bargainer I have ever seen. But I will steel myself to be like her and get the most for my money. Already we are hearing about the black market and the wonderful things we can buy from it, but at what prices! I will only buy what is absolutely necessary.

The toilets smell foul and I wish I had a handkerchief doused in perfume for every time I need to use it. I do not know how I will get used to this, but I imagine every person here said that to him or herself on their first day. I picture how a prisoner must feel, being shown his new confinement and I imagine this is not so very different. Linh cries as we walk through the camp. What did she imagine it would be like? I wish I could have talked to her about what our lives would be when we finished our sea journey, but I was focused on staying well and out of harm's way. And, I did not know myself. She must have envisioned a lovely place with gardens and swings, and a school with colorful pictures and storybooks. We were not even given the chance to pick the flowers on the shoreline.

My brother is very quiet, taking everything in. He is a deep thinker. I will speak in hushed whispers to him tonight about the money I have, how to stay together and how to watch out for each other here in this difficult place. I am glad and grateful there were no bad influences on our boat. I know how fourteen-year-old boys can be, but I can tell he took our father's words to heart. He is a good boy and he will help get us through this. It makes me feel guilty sometimes, thinking about what he might rather be doing. I would like to see him play a little, and will not discourage him from doing so, if there is the opportunity here in the camp. Perhaps there will be a place to play basketball, his favorite game.

Chapter 14

We awaken to the sound of screams coming from the shoreline. The sounds are muffled, but I know what they are. They cannot be disguised. The night is ink; the moon is new, keeping all its light to itself. My brother looks at me from his place on the long bed. We both look to our young sister. She is still asleep. She has been sleeping well since we have been here. I, on the other hand, sleep the light, disturbed sleep of a rabbit, always nervous, twitching, one eye open; as if I am prey waiting for the attack.

And something is wrong. Very wrong. But I dare not venture from the false safety of this hut. (Only a piece of string ties our door shut.)

We hear shouts and more screams and then we see lights moving in the darkness. Heading toward the beach. I see through our screen door as a guard roughly brings Old Man

Thanh back to his hut. I am relieved it is only he who is yelling and forcefully shaking his head. His habit is to walk at night. He, like so many of us, cannot sleep. But for him it is worse. He lost all his family, save one brother, to the war. Wife, children, grandchildren. They were in their village when the massacre took place. He came back from the rice fields to find them all dead. He barely speaks to anyone. Just walks and screams. No one talks about whether it was the Vietcong or the Americans who killed everyone. I think he will try to go to Australia.

But it seems it is not just the nightmares of Old Man Thanh. By now there is mayhem. Guards are telling people to stay in their huts, but this only makes them want to see what the old man was shrieking about. I hear running and then the sounds of more screams. Linh is awake now and crying. And then all the children in our hut are awake. I can no longer lie in my bed. I ask the mother of eight to stay while I go and see what is happening. I get up and shove my feet into my slippers, put my rough blanket about my shoulders, not for warmth, it is so hot, but for modesty, and follow the others out to the water's edge.

I make out shadows on the beach and I wonder if whales have beached themselves as I have heard they do at times. But on closer inspection, it isn't whales that line the sand, but poor dead Vietnamese, washed up on the shore. Bits of their tiny craft are broken on the beach. The guards are counting them with their flashlights. There are maybe thirty, so far. Who knows what will be washed in with the tide tomorrow?

I do not want to see their faces. It cannot be anyone from my family. It cannot. The man in white would never come so soon for the next group. But it has not been soon at all. It has been weeks. Of course now, I am certain he did come for them and a dreadful suspicion creeps into my being. I am praying that my third sister was not having a premonition the time she hid all day under my bed.

I sit down on the coarse sand, wrap my blanket tightly around me. The guards pay me no mind as they drag bodies and place them in a straight line, face up. They shine their flashlights onto this silent crowd, this still, motionless, bloated crowd, gathering face up on the sand. People are following the guards, searching for familiar faces and praying they do not find any they recognize. My brother is among the searchers, brave boy.

I am a coward. I cannot, will not, look. I just stare out to the dark blue sea, praying silently that I do not hear a sound from my brother. Not a word or a cry. He will return to me when he has found nothing we need to care about. I am crying freely now, but I do not want to care, cannot care.

Chapter 15

My brother did not find anyone of ours among the dead. They have been consumed by fire on the beach, a huge bonfire that might have seemed festive if it hadn't been so tragic. I have heard in Indonesia they burn their dead on pyres. That is not our way. But there was no place to bury them. And this government has no money to spend on burials for Vietnamese Boat People, as I have heard we are now called. I do not want to be known as a "Boat Person."

The smell of death still pervades the camp and no one walks near the beach. It has been cordoned off and there are guards with rifles standing nearby. I do not think they really need to be there. No one wants to go there. There are ghosts there now.

We have heard that if any more boats try to find safety on these shores, they will be shot on sight. I am always listening for the dreadful sound of gunfire. So far, things have been quiet.

Each day, I wait for an official to tell us it is time to go to our new home. That we can pack our bags and leave this place. I am trying to be patient, but it is difficult. I filed papers with the United Nations High Commission for Refugees, UNHCR, when we first arrived. I have asked that we go to New York, America, although where they send us is up to them. It could be anywhere in the world. But we do know someone there. In New York. It is the only place in the world we know anyone; a former colleague of my father's, and it is where my father told me to request. And so, it must be there that we are assigned. My father expects it. And when we get there, my task will be to sponsor the rest of my family. It is an awesome responsibility and I am so afraid I will fail. I have not wanted to think about it at all, and I will try not to think about it too much until it is necessary. I have so much else to think about. I have so many things to do. So many worries. I am trying to remain cheerful, but it is an act of will.

There is a little school here and both my brother and sister attend. It isn't much, just a shanty with some chairs and a chalkboard, but there are several kind Peace Corp workers who volunteer there. They live in the village near here and must show papers every time they come into the camp. There are two men and one woman, all English speaking, but I do not know from what countries they come. They sing songs with the little ones and try to teach all the children English, as they assume most of us will be leaving for English-speaking lands. This class is for children and I have too much to do during the day. I must practice on my own.

It may take weeks or months for our papers to be processed. The shortest time we have ever heard of is six weeks. Some people have been here for over two years now. Why do some get to leave, while others must remain? I pray that we are the lucky ones.

I am ready to start my life. I feel I am in limbo here, living for daily survival. Every day is the same. Sweep the dirt floor out into the dirt. Fold the blankets and place them neatly on the bed. Take the waste can we use at night to the latrine and dump it, holding my nose. Take some of my coins out of my hiding spot to buy rice. Collect sticks, start the fire. Prepare tea and gruel for our breakfast, rice for our lunch and supper. Sometimes I find a bit of meat or fish, a few vegetables. Some of the people who have been here for a long time have tried to grow vegetables in the dirt. A little cabbage, a few beans. They take coins for whatever they are willing to sell.

Pray each night to Kuan Yin.

I yearn to pick up a brush and dip it into velvety, rich colors. Touch it to a piece of soft rice paper. Watch something appear where there was nothing before.

I want to read a novel, with a smart and fierce heroine. One who wins the battles and is unafraid of anyone or anything. I want to do homework, writing down new English words and expressions that I can practice when I go to the market or walk down the street. I want to send my brother and sister off to school, wearing clean, pressed clothes, their hair smelling like American shampoo. I want to sit in a clean room on a comfortable chair and drink a cup of cà phê phin, and perhaps even eat a sweet mung bean cake at the same time.

I will wait with the patience of the hopeful, for that is all there is. Without it, I have nothing.

Chapter 16

The family we share our tiny hut with has received their papers and will be leaving for Australia in a short time. The mother cried, though from happiness or despair I could not tell. I cannot imagine anyone feeling sad or nostalgic about this place. Perhaps I will cry when we finally are able to embark upon the next leg of our journey, which hopefully will be our last. But I know I will cry from happiness. Wherever we are to go.

The children shouted and jumped up and down on our long communal bed and I became vexed thinking that they might break it. We still must sleep on it, with or without them.

I think my sister will be very sad to have them go. She has become friendly with them. They attend the little school together and play caps on our dirt floor. Sometimes she asks to change places with me on the long bed so that she can sleep between me and one of them, rather than in between me and our brother. She cuddles with one or the other of the little girls about her own age and they giggle under their covers. It feels like some kind of normalcy, so I consent to it, once in a while. I, too, am sad to see them go. The mother of the family and I, though not effusively friendly, and without much in common, have been neighborly and have bickered very little. At least we are now familiar with each other. I know the sleeping patterns of the family, their habits and routine. I wonder if a new family will come directly after this one leaves. Will the government let them in? If so, will they be friendly? From an educated home? Will there be a young man whom I must avoid?

At least we will be able to move further down the bed, away from the door.

My brother comes back from his lessons covered with dirt, a bruise starting to form over one eye, his face bleeding slightly. I have never seen him looking this angry before and I go to him, but he brushes me away. I ask him what has happened but he will not speak to me, so I leave him alone. Maybe later he will talk.

I go and pick up my sister who is still in the tiny shack with the volunteers and several other children. She runs to me and shows me a picture she has made. It is a boat with only three people on it and it is floating in a beautiful blue sea surrounded by a bright yellow sun and blue sky. There are birds in the distance. I know she did not draw all of it herself, and I look longingly at the colors on the paper. The volunteer is smiling and speaking to me, but I cannot understand what he is saying. Even if I had understood I am not paying attention. I am looking at the picture and thinking that I have not painted nor drawn anything since that day I buried my paints under the wisteria. I shake myself out of my reverie and compliment my sister on her lovely drawing.

I wish the volunteer would offer me the colored pencils and the paper, but he does not and I dare not ask. Or perhaps he did, speaking his strange words in the language I do not yet understand.

We walk slowly back to our hut and my brother is sitting on his section of the bed, his head down as if ashamed. I sit next to him, our knees barely touching and I whisper, asking him if he is ready to tell me what has happened. He nods his head and I see a tear fall onto his leg. It makes a spot on his cotton trousers. We both look at it for some time. He is about to speak when the family comes back. I notice little eight-year-old Phan looking admiringly at my brother.

My brother quickly wipes his face with his arm and I take his hand and lead him outside, leaving Linh playing with the little girls.

I ask him what has happened to cause him to fight. He tells me that one of the bad boys at school told little Phan that he'll be moving to a land of kangaroos and that he would start to hop like one and grow a pouch on his stomach once he got there. The little fellow became afraid and started to bawl. My brother tells the bully to stop telling lies. "Who's going to stop me?" he hollers at my brother. My brother tells him he will and that is when the bully hits him.

"Did you hit him back?" I ask him, secretly hoping he did.

Of course, my brother tells me. And the bully goes down like a sack of rice.

But my brother is crying again and I do not understand

why. We sit together on the worn out bench made of wood and metal, my brother crying while I pat his back and speak words of comfort. Is he guilty for hurting that mean boy?

When his tears are spent, he turns to me and says that he would give anything to leave this place, even if what the bully said was true. He wants to be part of Phan's family, the one that gets to go.

I tell him that we will be called soon. That he must be a little more patient. That the family we share our bed with has been here longer than we. That we will be lucky and say goodbye to this camp before long. By now I too am crying, my words of encouragement getting stuck in my throat. I too want to leave this sorry place and start my new life, even if it means going to someplace other than where I dream of going.

We walk back to our hut, my arm through his. We will leave soon. We have to be hopeful. My brother nods in agreement and we wipe our eyes before entering our tiny dwelling, where our sister is playing happily on the dirt floor.

Chapter 17

I am sick. We are all sick. I do not know what we are ailing from, but we crouch in our long bed and pull our knees up to our chests and cry from the pain. I want to care for my brother and sister, but I cannot, for I am sicker than they are. I cannot hold down even the blandest broth. My insides feel as if they were turning circles around each other and I cannot even get myself up to go to the latrine. The neighbors are saying dysentery or worms, probably from the water, which is undoubtedly contaminated.

I am afraid I will die and leave my poor siblings alone. I cannot. I must find strength to get well. The family living with us is leaving in a few days, but now I wish they would stay. The mother has been kind and is cooking soup and rice for us. None of her own is sick, but she cannot overlook us. I am grateful. She sent her oldest daughter to the field near the edge of the camp to gather leaves and flowers she thinks might help to cure us. I wish she would send for the doctor, but I am too weak to ask. My baby sister looks greener than when we were on the boat, but I notice she is eating a little congee. I thank Kuan Yin for that. My strong, brave brother writhes in pain and cries out for our mother.

And I, I feel flushed and hot and cold at the same time. My head spins and aches, throbbing as though my heart is beating in it. My stomach cramps like a fist and though there is nothing left to vomit, my body won't give up and I heave and retch and shudder, the taste in my mouth fouler than whatever poison I ate or drank.

When my mind is clear, I rebuke myself for my lack of dependability. I have tried to boil our water for more than the prescribed two minutes, but sometimes I forget and fill the tea pot as soon as the water roils and sputters.

Then I think, perhaps it is from the fish I bought on the black market the other day. I should have smelled it first, but the vendor said it was fresh. It looked fresh and I am so gullible. Oh, if only I had smelled it before I purchased it. Of course, I am sure now that it was off, but I so longed for a piece of fresh fish. I haggled harder than even my mother and spent our coins on it. Coins I could not spare. The man wrapped it in old newspaper and when I returned, I built a small fire and cooked it, pretending to myself that some fish smell fishier than others.

And I could not let my siblings go hungry. They are thin enough as it is. But oh, how I regret that decision now. We might all die due to my tightfistedness. If I was braver, I would have returned the rotten fish to him, but these traffickers are hard men. They care little for anyone's welfare, let alone a Chinese. And now we are sick, the odious contents of our stomachs leaving our bodies through every orifice. The stench of our hut is hard to take, and I am sure the family is desperate to be on their way to Australia.

Finally, I see a man in a white undershirt and shorts, rubber sandals on dirty feet. I later wonder how I even remember his appearance, but he is the doctor come to call and he gives us medicine which our kindly housemate gives us in mild tea, and soon we are feeling a little better.

When we are finally able to stand up, though our steps are wobbly and weak, the family leaves us. I cry freely as they make their way through the screen door and away from this place forever, weakly calling out my thanks. My emotions are willowy and fragile, and I am feeling a vulnerability I do not often feel nor reveal. But sickness and near-death can do that to a person, so I forgive myself. But I vow to return to my strength and swear to never again be fooled by anyone trying to take advantage of me. And I will boil our water for a full five minutes before brewing our tea.

Chapter 18

I thought we had seen the last of new arrivals, but the new ones who have just come are in worse condition than any we have seen. There has been another shipwreck, only this time there are survivors. A young girl is brought roughly to our hut by one of the guards, her clothes a sopping, ragged mess, her hair strewn about her gaunt face in wet, sticky clumps. She sits on the edge of our long slatted bed, dripping onto our dirt floor, silently sobbing while we stand around watching her, unsure of what has happened, unable to speak. She is twelve or thirteen, thin and weak, but the pain in her face makes her look many years older.

So many thoughts run through my mind as I watch her, longing to put my hand on her shivering shoulder, and give her words of comfort, though for what, I do not know. But that is not our way, and so I keep silent, the questions I want to ask kept to myself. But they spill from my mind, and I hope I can keep them in my mouth. I want to scream them, to ask her, did the pirates have their way with you, poor child? Was your boat pillaged? Did you witness things no child should bear witness to? But my mouth remains firmly closed and thankfully, I hold my tongue.

My brother is watching her as well, but he is smarter than I and gives her his rough blanket, putting it gently around her shoulders. She looks at the floor, but her head gestures slightly in acknowledgement. I am proud of my brother. He is kind and good. He is young, but he has taken his responsibility seriously.

I see her pull the blanket more firmly about her and then she begins to shiver in earnest. Her teeth are chattering, head bobbing, limbs twitching. It is not cold in our hut. No, it is scorching hot and humid. She is in a state of shock, I can see that now. Like in my friend's village, after a massacre by the Vietcong. People walked around like the dead, traumatized. I wish there was a doctor here, but no more boats were expected, and there is no doctor to care for us.

I don't know what to do, but I am determined to do something. I imagine she is my fifth sister and I go to her, whisper to her that she must lie down, and lead her into that position. She acquiesces and curls into the position of a babe inside its mother, her shivering growing stronger. I put my own blanket around her and run outside to start a small fire in the pit so that I can make soup for her to drink, to warm her.

Outside, as the flames of my tiny fire grow hot and I put water and what vegetables I can spare into my pot, I hear talk and I strain to listen. No wonder the girl is shaking and sobbing. The boat which carried her, her eighteen-year-old brother, their aunt and uncle, along with the twenty-nine others, sank just meters off shore from this island. She and her brother were the only ones able to swim to shore. Her brother, brave, brave boy, made sure she was safe, then swam out to rescue as many as he could, one by one, dragging them through the surf to the beach, leaving them and returning to the sea to get another. By the time he was finished he had rescued all those who were still alive in the water, which turned out to be only his aunt and eight others. He lay on the beach, gasping for breath, spitting salt water from his mouth. Suddenly blood started leaking from his eyes and ears, into his throat, where it choked him to death.

His little sister watched as he took his last, shuddering, bloodied breath.

I look at my pot full of water, tiny bubbles starting to form on the sides as the fire heats it up. I want to climb out of myself. I want to fly away, like I sometimes do in my dreams, and leave this place of despair, this place where a moment of hope seems to turn on itself and become anguish. I want my mother. I want my paints. A drop of water falls into the pot and I look up at the sky to see if it is raining. But the sun is hot and full. The sky surprisingly clear and blue. It is only me. The salty water leaking from my eyes into the soup pot. I didn't even know it.

Chapter 19

Our papers have been approved. My heart races and a smile starts to creep up onto my face, making the skin stretch. It has been months since I have smiled. The camp official called me into his office, which is nothing more than a shack with an old typewriter and a desk. I stood before this Malaysian officer, my heart pounding. He handed me some papers and spoke gruffly in very bad Vietnamese telling of our approval, but he gave me a very small smile and a nod before I left. I still do not know where we are to go, but we will be going somewhere soon. And anywhere will be better than here.

I do not know whether I should start to pack our things. It is probably best for me not to, as it could still take several weeks before we are assigned to leave. But I know the waiting will be impossible. I can barely think about it without having trouble taking a breath. I have not felt this excited in so long. I know it is anticipation mixed with fear, but right now, the expectation is paramount.

In a way I wish my young sister did not hear of it. Each day she asks me, "Mother, is this the day we are to go?" Each day I tell her no, not yet, soon. Each day her face falls. But I tell her not to fret. I tell her my secret dreams, the ones I think about while I prepare our meals or make our bed. They are fancies, simple flights of imagination. But they sustain me, and so I share them with her.

I tell her to close her eyes and envision us boarding the airplane, the kind pretty stewardess in her crisp, clean uniform happily leading us to our comfortable seats in the grand machine that will take us away from this place forever. I invite her to picture eating delicious food from a tray while looking out over the clouds from dizzying heights, of waving to any birds that might fly by. I ask her to decide what our new home will look like. For me, I see my new home with brightly colored curtains, soft beds with cool, soft sheets and an abundance of pillows that float under our heads like clouds. I tell her to see a kitchen which awaits us with plenty of fresh fruit and vegetables, fish and spices. I see a telephone to call my mother, whom I hope is still well, but I reserve that thought for myself. My sister smiles when I tell her these things. I can see she does this exercise often, as I catch her with her eyes closed and a smile about her lips, or I see her off in a daydream. I know where she is for I have been there many times myself.

And now, we are so very close to all the things I have only dreamed of that I can barely go about my monotonous routine without wanting to scream.

I must try not to be this way, but it is difficult. The day-to-day chores are mind-numbing and tedious. I have begun to burn the rice, so far away is my mind, what with imagining the packing and leaving, arriving in my new country, bathing in hot soapy water, sleeping in my soft bed until mid-morning. Each day that we hear no further news is like torture.

I try to occupy my time with my English books but it is no use. I cannot do it alone. And so I accompany my brother and sister to the shanty where they have their lessons. I pray to Kuan Yin that this English is useful, that we are sent to an English speaking land. I watch my brother and sister greet their instructors and I am ashamed that I have not yet learned even the simplest phrase. I tell myself I have been too busy collecting wood for the fire, haggling for our meager rations, keeping our clothes clean. But really, I have been afraid. Afraid to learn a language and be told we were assigned to a country that speaks another. Or maybe I am afraid to make friends that I will have to leave behind. I am not sure, but I am determined to say thank you to those who will help us make a new home.

The teacher smiles and seeing me hovering with no intention of leaving, invites me to join the group. I am the oldest one there, but I am past caring. Soon I will not have to see any of these people again and so I refuse to care about whether I will embarrass myself. I am here for one purpose.

The teacher points to himself and says, "Joe, Joe." He gestures to me and I announce my own name.

"Mei." I say it twice again and it sounds funny when he says it back to me.

"Maayyy."

Everyone laughs. He laughs along with us. It is a start.

Chapter 20

Thank you Kuan Yin! Thank you with all my heart. Our assignment came and we are to go to New York! America! The United States! My heart is soaring! My father will be overjoyed when I am able to finally contact him and tell him. My brother and sister and I danced around the dirt floor of our room while no one else was there.

I feel badly for our poor new housemates, with all their trouble and tragedy and wish they could accompany us, but they cannot and will have to wait for their own assignment. At least the girl and her aunt have each other, although the old woman seems not to be out of shock even after these many weeks. She walks around in a daze, unable to sleep at night, crying sometimes, wailing sometimes, smiling never. The girl is somewhat better, but not much. She refuses to attend the little school, even though I am now going and offer to bring her to every class. She sits on our long bed, holding her knees and rocks, back and forth. She must find solace in this movement. She likes to touch Linh's hair, petting it like a dog. Linh lets her do it, dear child, understanding that it is the only thing that gives the girl comfort. I hope she will be able to cope when we leave, which will be in only eleven days!

I bring all our clothes to the river and pound them with the biggest rock I can find, allowing myself to use more soap than usual. I do not want to look like a refugee when we arrive in New York. Who will be there to meet us? Will they speak Vietnamese? I can still only say a very few words in English. Just some greetings and numbers and how to say thank you. English is a very difficult language. The pronunciation is so strange to my tongue. But I suppose Vietnamese must be difficult to those who were not raised speaking it. Our teacher butchers our language every time he speaks, but at least he makes an attempt. I am sure I will do the same with English, massacre it, that is. I hope no one will laugh at me. But more than that, I hope I will be understood. I will study hard these last eleven days and I will enroll in an English class when I am settled in. My brother and sister have learned many words and expressions, but I do not know whether they will be willing to try to speak with anyone when we arrive. I hope their new teachers will be sympathetic.

How can we even wait eleven days? How will I be able to stand it? But we will fill our time with our studies and our packing, which I am sure we will do over and over again, arranging and rearranging. It almost seems ridiculous, we have so little. I have asked the volunteer teacher to work with me privately so that I can say more than simple words. My goal is to speak several sentences by the time we arrive and also to understand simple phrases.

We are to leave here and go to the large city nearby where there is an airport. We will fly from there to Hong Kong, where we will change planes for New York. We were told it would take several days from the time we leave to actually arrive in America. I do not care. As soon as we are off this island, away from this camp, I will feel like my new life will begin. I will feel free.

Chapter 21

We leave today. At one o'clock in the afternoon. I wash Linh's hair until it squeaks. It is longer now, black and thick and shiny. By the time we arrive, it will be in a sorry state, but I want to start our journey clean and ready. One of the volunteers gave her an old dress, which she begs me to let her wear. I do not know where they got the garment, and my irrational mind thinks it is probably from some child now dead, but I will not let my superstitions get in the way of her happiness, and so I wash the dress and let her wear it. Perhaps it is simply from a child who outgrew it and left it here when she herself left for her new country.

My brother washes his face until it nearly bleeds, and I wish I had an iron to get the wrinkles out of his clothes. I know we look ragged, but at least we will be clean. I wash my own hair, too. When it dries I pull my fingers through it many times, liking the soft cleanness of it.

How easy it is to leave this place. I thought that perhaps it would be a little difficult, but none of us sheds a tear as we walk through the door of our hut, bags in hand, and get into the jeep that will take us to the town with the small airport. And away.

For the journey, my neighbor, an old seamstress, gave me a needle, a small amount of thread, and a spare piece of cloth. I made a small waist belt and wear it under my shirt. Here I put our identification papers, the ones that say we are refugees. I put the meal vouchers I was given by the UNHCR official there, too. I will take no chances with our safety, with our journey to America, with our new start.

My sister is smiling as we board the small plane that will take us to Hong Kong. We, none of us, have ever been on an airplane before and Linh and I hold hands as the plane goes fast down the runway, causing our stomachs to surge and our bones to rattle. She is sitting by the window, calling me to look out as the craft lifts away from the ground and up into the air. My eyes have been tightly closed, a mantra on my lips. I open them to oblige her and see my brother, sitting on my other side, straining over me to look as well. We watch as the plane lifts, levels and turns, the mainland disappearing, the ocean, our lives in the camp, everything that was, becoming clouds, clouds becoming nothing but a white, wispy floor, all traces of what was, vanishing, gone.

I let out a breath that I realize I have been holding tightly to and it fogs the small window. Linh wipes it away quickly and I sit back in my seat, letting my sister have an optimum view of the vast nothingness that surrounds us. It is clean. It is huge and open and new. It has no past, only present and future. I see her reflection in the glass as she looks out, her wonder at what is there and what lies ahead.

A lovely Malaysian woman in a crisp blue uniform brings us soft drinks and salted nuts. We look at them as though we had never seen anything like them before, like we are peasants from the countryside. But we have tasted soft drinks before. We have eaten nuts. We had a life before. A good one, for part of the time.

Then I remember and realize that my young sister has never experienced what was truly happy and good in Vietnam. She was born only four years ago, into a war-ravaged country, into a Chinese family. I open the can of soda for her and I watch her eyes bulge as the sweetness of it spills onto her taste buds. Tuan drinks his in a few gulps, but the beverage is too sweet for me, too cloying, and I let them finish it. When the woman returns to retrieve our empty cans I ask for a glass of water. I want something clean and pure.

We arrive in Hong Kong as evening falls and it is as if we are flying over a magical realm. Colored lights sparkle over the water from buildings as high as clouds. Boats fill the harbor that we pass as the plane circles it, getting ready to land.

Linh is asleep, but I wake her as we fly over this wonderland and she pulls herself out of slumber and into this waking dream. I have never seen anything so beautiful and I wish we could be tourists, being greeted by friends or family, led to a fine hotel, fed a sumptuous Chinese meal. But we are refugees with meal vouchers, who must stay within the confines of the airport for many hours while we wait for our next flight which will take nearly a full day.

We walk around the airport, hearing people speaking in Cantonese, a language we speak fluently, our other tongue which by now has surely become rusty. I long to talk to someone, but what would I say, I have no friends here, no relations. But I do have meal vouchers, so I take my brother and sister to a food stall within the airport and I order our meal, the language sounding at once familiar and strange as I speak with this Chinese stranger. We are given a full meal, including rice, soup, meat and noodles. Even this airport food is delicious. It is plentiful and tasty and I want to go on eating even after I am full, it has been so long since we have eaten this much, but I cannot. My stomach is so shrunken that it hurts.

We walk around the airport and look out the huge glass windows watching airplanes take off, and we wonder where they are going. Are there people like us on board? Will they be greeted by relatives, friends?

"Who will greet us?" my small sister asks. I wish I had an answer, but I do not. I can only hope someone will be there when we arrive after this long and tiring journey. But I tell my sister that of course some kind person who knows we are coming will be waiting for us. I hope I am correct.

"Will there be a sign with our name on it?" she asks, her face lighting up. "Like the ones we have seen today at the gate when we arrived?" Of course, I tell her and hope that this too, is true.

Several hours later, we are ready to board the large aircraft which will be the last part of the journey. We are very tired, but we are too excited to sleep right away. There are meals to eat off plastic trays with chopsticks wrapped in paper. There are films to watch and music to listen to. I begin to feel civilized again. The plane is filled with mostly Chinese, but few or no refugees, or so I can tell. As I walk to the restroom, I glance discreetly at my fellow passengers. Everyone I see looks tidy and well dressed. No one looks like us. I do not walk to the restroom too many times.

Linh curls up in a ball and sleeps for hours, hours which go on and on, time turning circles on itself. My watch still hangs from my wrist, but tells me nothing. I learn from the pilot, speaking English and Chinese, that we have crossed the International Dateline and we are going backwards in time. It is yesterday. I am not sure if this is a good omen or a bad one. Perhaps it is neither. My brother and I try to sleep once the films are over and we have exhausted the music on our headphones. We doze on and off, waking each other constantly to ask where we think we might be in the world. We lift our window shade open and look once out onto a night sky accented only by the blinking lights of the plane, once onto a pink and shimmery sunrise, and finally onto a bright sunny day, the beginning of our descent. We are all awake as we watch as buildings come into view. Tall towers take up most of the landscape, a river under several wide, long bridges, tiny trees devoid of all color. I think I see that most famous, welcoming structure of New York and I tell my sister and brother to look in that direction. The plane lands with a thud that makes us catch our breath and plug our ears as the craft pulls to a stop, the noise and speed dizzying.

And soon I know that I have told my sister the truth, for when we do arrive at John F. Kennedy International Airport some thirty hours after our Chinese meal, I see a sign with our surname on it, Phoung, and I begin to cry. My tears escape before I have any control over them. I walk slowly toward the sign, my sister's tiny hand in mine, my brother at my side, both of us carrying our small bags. A smiling gray-haired American woman puts the sign down and comes forward as she sees us coming towards her. She greets us in Vietnamese, Chinese and English, and I allow myself to fall into her arms, allowing her to hug me, the warmth of her greeting overwhelming me.

"Welcome," she says in our language, and I believe she truly means it.

Part 2

Hannah

Chapter 22

High school is the bane of my existence. Truly. I hate it. I mean, really hate it. My teachers are awful, the classes are boring and I have no friends. Lunchtime is the worst, especially in winter. And except for lunch, because I can't eat outside by myself, I love winter. You know, you've seen the pictures of the one kid out on the school lawn under a tree. That's me. And it's fine, except in winter. In winter I've got to go somewhere during that thirty seven minute endless stretch of time that is called "lunch period."

So I go into the library and try to eat in the stacks, but the librarian always catches me. She hates me, I know. That's because last year they weren't going to let me graduate from tenth grade unless I paid some overdue fine. I swear I had returned those books, but no, no passing until the fine was paid. So I brought in a brown paper bag full of pennies, and plopped it right on her desk. It was all there, every greasy cent of what she said I owed. Legal tender. Anyway, now she has it in for me. So my one safe haven is now off limits. I can't eat in the halls. My guidance counselor always seems to find me.

"Hannah? Hannah?"

I pretend not to hear her.

"Hannah!"

"Um, yeah?" I look up innocently at her from the book I'm reading.

"Hannah, what are you doing?"

What does it look like I'm doing here chewing and swallowing?

"Huh? Oh, just waiting for Mr. R. to come back. I've got a science assignment I need help with." I look really innocent, I think.

"Hannah, you know the rules. No eating in the halls. C'mon, let's go to the cafeteria."

She extends her hand to me, but I shove the rest of my apple into my mouth and get up quickly, grab my books and head in the other direction. I know she's still standing there, watching me, shaking her head. She can't figure me out. And that's fine with me. No one needs to know me, anyway.

People used to know me. Quite well as a matter of fact. I used to have friends. I had quite a goodly number of them. I had a best friend and lots of second and third best friends, too. But something happened when we entered this place; this overwhelming, conformist prison called high school. Drugs and the Grateful Dead. All my friends started smoking pot and listening to Jerry! Some of them even started smoking cigarettes, which was almost worse than the grass. I didn't want any of it and I sure wasn't going to pretend to like the Dead. I went to the parties for a while, but I never enjoyed them. I'd just sit and pet the dog, if there was one, and miserably watch everyone having fun. Once, and I swear this is true, having witnessed it with my own eyes, they actually bowed before the speakers when Jerry Garcia started to sing. They'd pass the pipe or the joint and I'd refuse. That's when they dropped me. Even my best friend Amy dropped me like a hot potato and we'd been best friends since fourth grade! I can talk about it now, but it hurt like hell. They all dropped me. Every stinking one of them.

Once, this girl, Tammy, came up to me in the hall and actually whispered, "Some of us respect you, Hannah, for doing your own thing, but if you're not with us, we can't be friends with you."

I stood there for a long time, not wanting to believe that they wouldn't be friends with me anymore because I wouldn't conform to their ideas. How incredibly superficial! They used to want to be things like veterinarians or teachers, environmental scientists or writers. I still do. I don't get it.

And then they just got mean.

Last year Amy pretended to be my friend again, and sucker that I am, Miss Gullible, I believed her. She said,

"David Rickman likes you, Hannah. He told me."

David Rickman was the most gorgeous boy in tenth grade. I'd had a crush on him since eighth grade and she knew it. I wanted to believe her. I tried to look good; I smiled at him when I saw him in the halls. I cringe recalling the humiliation. I even tried to talk to him in our one class together, photography, at which I can honestly say, I am the best in the class. I thought he admired my prints and me and I stupidly thought he acted interested. And pathetically, I really believed Amy when she told me he wanted me to meet him at the bleachers after school. What a sucker.

I went there, wearing the prettiest blouse I had. I had just bought it at this new Indian boutique. I had my hair in loose braids, my new lace-up Earth shoe boots under my bells.

He was there waiting for me.

And so was Amy and Tracy and Lauren, and God, I don't even remember who else. They were laughing. The last thing I saw before I ran home was Amy sitting on his lap, her head thrown back, laughing out loud. I stayed home from school for two days after that, pretending to be sick. But I wasn't really pretending. I was sick and hurt and totally humiliated. I can never forgive them for what they did.

So now it's just me and my Pentax 35mm camera my dad bought me before I went to the Grand Canyon. It's my constant companion. Behind the lens, everything looks different, clearer. People think I'm weird and I get lots of threatening looks whenever I take a candid shot, but I can see what people are really like when they come out of the developer and onto my paper.

I've been seeing my old therapist. The same one I used to see when I was eight and my grandmother had just died. Boy did that mess up my head. I used to be sick everyday for just about all of second grade. I went to the school nurse every morning to try and get her to call my mother to pick me up. Every day it was something else; a stomachache, a sore throat, a headache. My mother took me to the doctor who told me I wasn't really having stomachaches or sore throats at all. That it was all in my mind. He actually used the word psychosomatic to an eight year old! I remember screaming and saying I really did have a stomachache. I really did.

Anyway, I think my mother's crazy to waste her money on this shrink. There's nothing wrong with me. Just because I don't smile, have no friends, and am angry all the time, doesn't mean I need to see a shrink.

At least my mother lets me take her car.

Mrs. Rosenkrantz, with her Sigmund Freud accent, invites me in and always asks so many questions, practically badgers me, until I can't stand it. I tell her about Mr. Meandro, my geometry teacher from last year. I despise him. Loathe him. He is a supreme bastard. He is despicable. His name should just be the first four letters. He failed me. He knew I was a math moron and he made me come up to the board and write theorems when he knew full well that I had no idea what I was doing. He stood there, arms folded across his chest, leaning against the board, watching me squirm with this self-satisfied expression on his face. At first I thought he was anti-Semitic and he was being a racist. Then I found out he was half-Jewish, by his mother, making him Jewish according to that law. So I guess he just hated me in general.

I ask her why a teacher would do that. She shrugs. Now I have to retake geometry. At least this year I have Mr. Lorie. He's new and cool with long hair and a beard and he seems really excited about teaching. But I don't mention this to Mrs. R.

She knows about my friends or lack thereof, but every week she asks a million questions about why I refused to try pot or cigarettes. Why I hated parties. I can tell she thinks I'm one weird kid. I tell her I'm a non-conformist. That even my own mother thinks I'm weird. My mother actually asked me if I wanted to try pot. I told her to lay off. It wasn't my scene. How difficult is that to understand? I wish I grew up in the sixties. I was born into them, but was too young to be a part of them. No one would look cross-eyed at me if this was 1968 instead of 1977. In the sixties you could just be yourself, whatever that meant.

I let my shrink know that my two sisters aren't perfect goody-two-shoes either, thank the Lord, and I make sure they don't conform. Ruthie, the middle one, twelve, started wearing makeup, but I put a stop to that. I told her the truth, that she looked like a jerk and would become a slut with all that stuff on her eyes. She cried and told our mother, who told me to mind my own business. I feel like if she wasn't going to say anything to her daughter, I'd better. Mrs. Rosenkrantz gives me a weird look when I tell her this bit of information. She probably agrees with my mother.

Joni, my little sister is almost nine years younger than I am and at almost eight years old, she's still moldable. I've been trying to tell her about animal rights and the plight of the American Indians. She seems to get it, she even told me we shouldn't eat meat, but then she just goes back to playing with her Barbies. It's a real drag.

Mrs. R. tells me I still look too thin. I tell her I gained two pounds since I last saw her. That's huge for me. A year and a half ago I stopped eating. Just about completely. I thought maybe if I was skinny, I'd get a boyfriend. Not that I was fat. So I started eating 800 calories a day. I memorized the entire calorie counter I got at the supermarket checkout line.

Every day it was the same. One hard boiled egg for breakfast, a plain yogurt and a red Delicious apple for lunch, and then a tiny piece of whatever meat my mother cooked and a teaspoon or two of vegetables. No dessert, no snacks. I have amazing willpower and, of course, the weight started dropping off. It was fun for a while, all my mother's friends commenting,

"Ooh, Hannah, you've lost all your baby fat…"

"Wow, you'll be able to fit into that bikini this summer…"

"Oy, I'm so jealous…"

Fun, that is, until I lost my period. Not that I enjoyed having it, although I have to say, I hardly get cramps, but I had just gotten it two years before, so having it disappear didn't seem like a good thing. Fun, that is, until I would cry at night from hunger pain. My stomach would hurt so badly I couldn't sleep. I remember one night calling my mother to come into my room because I was in such pain. I thought I was going to die. I think I was starving to death. I'm sure I was. My mother knew it, too, and begged me to eat. But I couldn't.

I used to look in the mirror at least fifty times every day, and see a chubby girl standing there. Everyone else saw a bony, practically emaciated me, but I saw a fat girl and was disgusted with myself. Even though everyone told me I was skinny enough and had better stop dieting, I couldn't.

And then one day I just got so cold. I was sitting at the table doing my homework. My mother was in the kitchen cooking and ready to help me if I needed it like always, and suddenly my hands got freezing and turned blue. I swear to God. They were ice cold and bright blue. My mother got hysterical, and so did I. She called my dad and they took me to the doctor who did all kinds of tests. He told me I was anemic and had Anorexia Nervosa. He told me it was a kind of mental illness. That's right, mental. And that if I didn't start to eat, he'd hook me up to an I.V. or I'd die. Like that made me feel better!

Anyway, that doctor scared the crap out of me. I didn't want to be insane, mentally disturbed. And that's when my mother made me see my old shrink.

And my therapist hasn't let up about this issue. It was so hard to eat at first. It still is. At the beginning, I could barely take two bites of food without wanting to throw it all up. But now I keep thinking about the I.V. or death, so I try to eat a little more every day.

There was one girl in my sophomore class, Lena, who used to bring me Ring Dings and Yodels. Maybe she knew what I was going through, I don't know. She was actually nice to me, but I was still so raw from being dumped that I treated her like garbage until she finally backed off. I'm sorry about that now.

Anyway, I tell Mrs. R. I'm almost back up to a hundred and five pounds. I don't look that bad anymore. I even cut my hair for the first time ever, and the guy gave me bangs. I'm still trying to get used to them. My hair is no longer down to my waist, but pretty close.

She asks me if there is anything that makes me happy these days. Happy? I have to think about that one. It's hard to say, I tell her. Then I remember things that make me feel better. Yeah, a few things, I tell her. Number one, James Taylor. He is my savior. Whenever I'm pissed off, which is most of the time, I just go into my room and put any of his records on, and then I'm all right. I've got all of them. Every one.

Number two: Animals are the other things that make me feel okay. I want to be a vet, I tell her. I've rescued and rehabilitated about a dozen squirrels and a few birds that my cats have gotten hold of.

What's number three? my shrink asks. She doesn't miss a trick. Writing, I tell her. I wrote my first book when I was five. Stinky Skunk Sees His Shadow. I used to show my work to people. Teachers and stuff, but I don't anymore.

Why? she asks, as if she actually gives a damn.

I tell her I wrote a story in seventh grade. It was an assignment and the teacher said to write whatever we wanted. I wrote a story about a dolphin who rescued a human from drowning. At first she gave me an "A" and told me it was the best piece of writing she'd ever seen from a seventh grader. The next day she told me she'd thought about it and she thought I might have gotten the idea from someone else. She asked me if I knew what plagiarism was. Of course I did, I told her. And then she accused me of it! I told her to go and find the original if she could. I really wanted to tell her to go to hell. Even my mother had a conference with her. At the end, she figured out that I really had written it, but she never apologized and that was it for me. So now I only write for myself.

I like to lie on my bed, listen to JT, and write stories of all kinds. But I'm the only audience now, I tell her.

That's a shame, my shrink says. She says she'd like to see some of my writing. Like that's ever gonna happen.

Anything else? she asks, looking at the camera hanging from my neck, her eyebrows going up a bit. I hold it up as if to take her picture. She puts her hand out and covers her face. I don't take it, but I tell her about it. She nods her head as if she understands and asks if she can see some of my work. Maybe, I tell her.

It's not too bad, seeing my old shrink. At least she seems interested in what I have to say. Nods in all the right places. And I always tell her way more than I ever intended. But it doesn't mean I'm going to get happy so quickly. Like I said, high school is my living hell and the sooner I get through it, the better I'll be.

Chapter 23

"I'm going to a rally in New York City next Saturday," I tell my mother who is cutting string beans on the counter.

"What kind of rally?"

"Save the seals. Do you know what they're doing to baby seals in Canada?"

"I'm sure you'll tell me."

"They're clubbing them for their fur. They have this soft white fur only when they're babies and they're so helpless. They're easy targets." It's true and sickening. It's my latest cause. I've already raised fifteen dollars for Greenpeace. I want to become a Greenpeace worker and go out on those Zodiacs and stop the Russians from killing whales and fight those Canadian hunters who are clubbing the seals! I don't understand the human race.

"That's horrible!" my mother agrees. I knew she would.

"Yeah. They use that fur for muffs and collars. It makes me sick! Greenpeace volunteers are going out onto the ice in Canada and spray-painting their fur! Isn't that great?"

"Sounds kind of mean."

"Mom, don't you get it? If they do that, their fur is worthless. God, I wish I could do that! So, can I go?"

"What! To Canada?"

Really! "Mom! To the rally!"

"Who are you going with? Are you going with a group?" my mother asks hopefully. She'll let me, I know it, because to her, even a radical group is better than none at all.

"No, I'm just gonna take the train myself. The rally is near Grand Central. I'll be fine."

"How did you find out about this anyway? Are any of your friends going?"

I roll my eyes. What friends? I know what she's trying to find out. Have I finally found a kindred spirit? An actual friend?

"No, Mom. I got a newsletter from Eco-Defenders."

I can tell my mother is disappointed, but she says yes anyway.

"I think Ruthie would love to come," she adds innocently. I wasn't expecting this.

"I truly doubt it, Mom. She's not very political."

"What do you expect, she's only twelve. I still think you should ask her."

"Yeah, sure. I will. Could you lend me some money? I won't get paid 'til next week."

"How much?"

"I don't know, train fare and some money for food.

Especially if Ruthie is coming."

I have a job as a "page" at the local library. I think it's a great title for someone who works with books, even though my job has to be the least glamorous one in the library. I'm the one who re-shelves the returns. I like it 'cause no one bothers me and I love sitting on the floor putting away my stack of 851.2s or 319.6s and trying to imagine what kind of person takes out books on travel to New Zealand or basic canoeing techniques. I asked for Saturday off before I even asked my mother, but I knew my mother would say yes. As suburban as she is, my mother still has a radical streak in her, maybe left over from the 60's. She married my father quite young, when she was only 21, and put away Bob Dylan for my father's preference of Mozart, Mozart and more Mozart. She's beautiful and still young, which makes me feel relieved. She's only 38 years old, and I sometimes calculate how old she'll be when I'm twenty-five or forty. Some of my classmates have parents in their fifties! I think about how old they'll be when their kids graduate college or how old they'll be in the year 2000. I'm glad my mother had me young.

The bright yellow wall phone rings shrilly and I pick it up. "Hellllooo!" It's Poppy, my grandfather. He says hello as if he were calling from some incredible distance, like the Swiss Alps every time he calls, almost yodeling.

"Hello, Poppy!"

"Is that my Hannah banana?"

How long is he going to call me that ridiculously obvious name? "Yes, of course, can't you tell my voice?"

"Of course I can! Something's coming soon, remember? Well, I just might have something for the big event."

"What's coming soon? Are you adopting a baby?" I always tease him. Poppy married Helen a few years after Nanny died. She's a retired vaudevillian actress of Irish descent, who always talks about the fact that she wanted children, but her previous husbands (emphasis on the plural) had never wanted any. She considers my mother her daughter, though I'm not sure my mother feels the same. But she's like a grandmother to us and we love her like she is.

My birthday is still a month away, but Poppy always discusses it before it comes. Every year he gives me and my sisters the worst, cheapest gifts. I can just imagine what he has for me this year.

"No, my gorgeous daughter and you three are enough for anyone!"

"So what could possibly be that special?"

"You know what it is! How old are you going to be this year, twelve?"

"Very funny! You know very well I'll be seventeen."

"And I've got in my hands the key to your happiness!" he says, emphasizing the word "key." No way, I think, my heart speeding up. It couldn't be what I'm suddenly praying it is! Every year he gives me junk jewelry, record albums from the fifties, an old scrapbook with no scraps in it, only yellowing paper. He's a dentist and thinks gift-giving means giving us the little plastic rings he gives out to his patients. Forget it; I'm not getting my hopes up. It's probably just the key to an old jewelry box or a suitcase. Maybe he's planning to take me on a trip to the Catskills where he and Helen love to go to those Jewish resorts. God, I hope not.

I went there once with my parents and had the worst time.

They forced me to go to the youth dance where nerdy looking teenage boys and overly made-up girls stood around listening to some kind of horrible music from another era, probably played for the benefit of the chaperones. My lucky sisters got to go to the pool while I was in agony, standing around that stupid dance, waiting until the allotted amount of time passed that would satisfy my parents.

No, Poppy isn't that evil. But if it is a car, it definitely wouldn't be a new one. What I really want is a Morris Mini. I saw the Beatles driving one and it was the cutest thing ever. But besides the fact that they're not sold in America, that isn't likely to happen! My grandfather is the cheapest man alive. It's probably his old white Dodge. The one he's had for 16 years. Which he probably bought used. But beggars can't be choosers, and driving that would be better than driving my mother's boat of a station wagon when she lets me.

"Poppy, don't tease me. What is it?"

"Nuh uh uh. Let me speak to my daughter."

"Poppy!"

"Goodbye, Hannah banana! See you on the freeway!"

At that moment my father comes in the back door, loosening his tie. He grabs my mother from behind and kisses her on the neck. She turns to kiss him, holding the phone away from her ear. I wish I had my Pentax on me. It grosses my sisters out, but I like it when I see my parents loving like that and I'd like to capture it on film. The moment is gone, and my father kisses the top of my head as he goes into the living room to pour himself a drink.

Chapter 24

I got a "D" on my Social Studies paper. It was titled "Theories of the Bering Strait," and it was based on the theory that American Indians originally came from Asia about twenty-five thousand years ago by way of the frozen land bridge. I researched the damn thing, I had footnotes and a bibliography and everything, but my dolt of a teacher gave me a "D" because he said there were no facts! Duh! It was a theory! Based on evidence, which my paper supported! How am I going to get into college if I get grades like these? And believe me, I want to go to college. I want to get out of here! I was thinking College of the Atlantic in Maine where they converted old chicken coops and turned them into dorms. I think that is so cool. I'll study environmental science there.

Amy got an "A" on her paper, which she showed her friends, glancing smugly in my direction. Her paper was about Abraham Lincoln. How easy is that to write? I'm sure she just copied it out of the encyclopedia. I am not meant for this school. There must be some way out of here. I wonder what I did to be so unjustly punished that I have to spend my days like this, tortured, surrounded by people who know nothing, care about nothing.

I do admit, I have one great teacher. Mr. Rizzo. Riz. He drives a Triumph convertible and is so fat he can barely fit in it, but he loves it and doesn't care what anyone thinks of him. He teaches science and he lets me help him in the class. During vacation I take home his snakes and gerbils. Last year one of the gerbils gave birth and my cat got hold of one of the many babies. I took the poor thing to the vet, who thought I was nuts. The baby gerbil died anyway, but the vet still charged me. Riz was mad at the vet when I told him. When I'm a vet, I won't charge people if their animals die in my care.

Riz is practically the only one who makes my day bearable. He reads us a passage from a book called, "The Day of Saint Anthony's Fire," about a village in France that ate bread made with moldy dough and everyone had LSD-like visions and hallucinations. People went crazy in this little town. Even a cat that had eaten some of the bread climbed up the wall, literally. And people think I'm weird for not smoking grass or dropping acid!

I can tell no one appreciates Riz like I do. He is weird and interesting. They just make fun of his blubber, but I see beneath it. I just wish he'd lose weight so maybe some woman would appreciate him. I think he's very lonely, but who knows? Then again, I lost weight and no one likes me. Maybe my theories really aren't worth more than a "D."

I caught my sister Ruthie and her friend Kay trying cigarettes in the churchyard after school the other day. I nearly went crazy. "Don't you know that Nanny died from smoking!" I told her. "I'll kill you if you do it again and I'll tell Dad!"

I don't think she'll do it again any time soon, not after I got through with her. Why would she do something so stupid? To be part of the crowd? She's mostly mad because she thinks Kay won't be her friend anymore because of me. I'm sick of everyone trying to please the crowd. Screw the crowd! That's my motto. Screw them all!

I pierced my own ear yesterday. Joni Mitchell was playing on my record player when I did it. Blue. I'll never forget it as long as I live. The left side. Second hole. I froze it with an ice cube and then stuck the needle, which I burned with a match to sterilize it, into my ear. I held half an apple on the other side. I actually got it right where I marked it. It hurt like crazy and I tried not to cry. I felt myself floating up and I thought I was going to pass out. I put my gold stud in, the one I used when I got my ears pierced on my 14th birthday, but by the time I got it almost all the way through, the back had closed slightly and I heard this pop as I pushed. I almost threw up. I put Neosporin around it and twirled it. Now I can't stop twirling it. Round and round. When my father sees it, he's gonna go nuts. He thought getting it done the first time was "barbaric." I convinced my mother to do hers at the same time I did when she took me. You should've seen my dad when he noticed her studs! He just shook his head, back and forth, looking disappointed, which of course makes everyone feel worse than his anger does. His anger explodes quickly and then it's gone. But the disappointment, that just lingers and festers and makes everyone feel terrible. But sorry, Dad, this is for me. Nobody else. Nobody'll even notice.

Actually that's not true. There is this one guy who notices me. He's very nice, but not very good-looking. He's always involved in the school musicals and I think he writes his own music. I think he likes me, but I have no attraction for him whatsoever. That just figures, doesn't it? The only boy in the entire high school who has the even slightest interest in me and he doesn't do it for me in the least. I did sit with him at lunch the other day. I looked over and saw Amy give her friends a self-satisfied look. Oh, pity poor Hannah sitting there with geeky Richard. I just smiled and took her picture. I know she hates when I do that.

I almost thought about going out with him as a statement, but I didn't want to hurt him by leading him on. So now I have a friend. It's good to have someone to eat with, especially in the winter.

Chapter 25

The train to Grand Central is almost empty when Ruthie and I leave for the rally. She waves crazily from the platform to our father who smiles and waves from the open car window. My father is so crazy for the cold; he drives with his window wide open, even in the dead of winter! Anyway, she's never been to the city before without our parents. Not that I'm such an old pro at it, but going to Grand Central isn't such a big deal. The subway is another story. Even I'm not ready for that yet.

We arrive in the city and walk the few blocks uptown to a big department store where the rally is being held. There are dozens of people standing outside in the freezing morning, bundled in parkas, holding signs with slogans like "Enjoy your fur, its real owner was killed in it" or "Save the Seals." One girl is wearing a scarf of naked, bloody, baby dolls. I am really impressed. I hope everyone gets the point.

Somebody hands us anti-fur slogans on sticks and we go and stand with the rest of the crowd and block people as they try to make their way into the fancy, establishment department store. It's organized and I don't feel like I'm the only one in the world with any convictions. I take a couple of pictures of the protesters and nobody objects.

Some of the protesters are calling out nasty things to the shoppers. Ruthie looks at me, like I'm the one who's saying it. I can tell she doesn't like this, but she doesn't say anything. I'm not leaving, no matter what she wants to do. She didn't have to come along in the first place.

A woman in a fur coat is looking extremely agitated as she tries to get past the crowd. Someone yells, "Enjoy your fur, maybe you're wearing somebody's mother!"

The woman gives the demonstrator a dirty look and tells him to mind his own business. He calls out, "It is my business! It's everybody's business! Don't you know how they got the coat you're wearing? Slaughter!"

The woman clutches her bag tightly to her chest and runs inside the store. I suddenly imagine my own mother trying to shop here and how I'd feel if someone yelled at her like that. One of the organizers is handing out sticky cards with some anti-fur slogan on it that we're supposed to stick on any unsuspecting passersby who happen to be wearing fur. I don't think I want to do that. A bunch of people start walking in a procession holding a small coffin. Inside, there's a toy baby seal, made to look as if it is covered in blood. I can see Ruthie is getting freaked out.

"Hannah, can we leave? I don't like this."

"C'mon, Ru. These people need to know what's happening to the seals and the rest of the animals they're wearing." I try to say this with conviction, but I'm a little grossed out, too.

"I'm afraid we're gonna get in trouble," she says, looking over to see an approaching squad car making its way to where we're gathered.

"This is legal and we're not hurting anybody. You know, free speech, freedom of assembly. That's all we're doing. Relax."

"Yeah, kid. We've got to get a message to the establishment!" says some eavesdropping protestor wearing a sign around his neck.

Ruthie rolls her eyes at me.

"Ruthie, I'm staying until this is over. Don't be such a baby."

The police car circles our rally, letting off blips of his siren, trying to scare us. It makes me mad, which gives me courage to keep protesting. I try not to think about what the cop might do. We stay for another hour or so, until we're too cold to keep it up. We made our point.

"Let's get some hot cocoa." I'm sure Ruthie is freezing and I kind of feel bad for her and I'm proud of her too. She really was scared but she kept her sign up high.

There's a diner nearby and we sit at a booth looking out onto the street. After our hot chocolate comes, we sit and watch a Chinese man (I guess he's Chinese although I'm really not sure) selling some trinkets on the street. A crowd is gathering around him. He's demonstrating a flying toy bird and people are handing him money for them. He hands the little kids the toys after he gets his money and the kids look thrilled. Then, the same cop who'd been circling us, goes up to the guy, demanding something. Probably a license. The poor man looks helplessly at the cop, but I can see the cop couldn't care less. He just writes out a ticket and hands it to the guy. The man looks miserable, but he packs up his stuff and gets out of there, quick.

"Can you believe that!" I say angrily. I am blowing so hard on my cocoa that it sprays on the table.

"Well, the guy probably wasn't supposed to be there."

"Ruthie, he was trying to make a living. He wasn't hurting anybody. He was making people happy, in fact."

"Hannah, could I get a piece of that Boston Cream Pie?" Ruthie asks, pointing to the revolving dessert tray, changing the subject.

"Didn't Mom give you any money?"

"Nope, she said she gave it to you. So, can I?"

"I guess so."

I watch her eat the pie, wishing I had some kind of appetite, because the pie looks good. I really am trying to eat a bit more, but it's hard.

We ride home on the train, but I am still thinking about the seals and the Chinese man and so I keep quiet. I know Ruthie was hoping we'd do something else, like go sightseeing, but I'm in no mood for any fun. I'm in a bad mood now. Thank goodness Ruthie brought her pad and markers. She can draw and leave me alone.

We pull into the train station and call home for a ride. It's cold as we stand on the platform waiting for our father to pick us up.

"Hannah."

I don't even hear her until she is yelling my name.

"Hannah, are you deaf?!"

"Sorry, I was thinking. What is it?"

"Nothing, never mind."

"Don't. What were you trying to say?"

"I was wondering if you wanted to play 'English Girls?'"

We haven't played this in a long time. It's this game that I made up where we pretend to be tourists from England. We have to speak in English accents and the first one who slips back into American, loses. I always win. I have the best accent. I haven't played in years, and I don't want to play now. I can tell Ruthie is disappointed and I'm glad when I see Dad waving at us out of the window of his hideous 1969 Cadillac DeVille.

Chapter 26

"You look like a refugee from a rummage sale!" my mother screams at me from the top of the stairs. "You are not leaving the house looking like that!"

I cannot stand this! "Let me dress the way I want to! How does it possibly affect you?"

"Your father is a prominent member of the community and I won't have you wearing rags!" she tells me, like I care. What does my father's job have to do with me? He's the head lawyer for our whole town, and I think his job is more important to my mother than it is to him.

"Like anyone in town even knows who I am in relation to him! What do you think I'm going to do anyway, barge into his office and show his clients my latest thrift shop find? Give me a break!"

I shop at the Salvation Army and the two other thrift

shops in town. I get my flannel shirts, my jeans and other cool stuff there. And it's cheap!

My mother wants to take me shopping at Macy's or Bloomingdale's, tries to bribe me into going, but I really don't care to spend any time or money in those conformist establishments.

I wash my used clothes after I buy them. I've found some hip clothes on many occasions. At least I like them. My mother can't stand the fact that I wear hand-me-downs, as she calls them. "You are the oldest! Your sisters should be wearing your hand-me-downs!"

But I know the score. As soon as we get home from a shopping trip to her fancy department store and my father sees the bill, there's the inevitable fight.

"Did you even look at the tag before you bought this!" he'll yell. And she'll scream back, "Why must you be so cheap! I want my children to look good, not like ragamuffins!" And he'll scream, "And you had to go to the most expensive store in town! You couldn't have gone to Rodney's?" Yeah, like my mother would ever go to that schlock house. But this is coming from a man who used to wear maroon pants, a red checkered shirt, and a paisley tie, until my mother couldn't take it anymore and started shopping for him.

As far as I'm concerned, thrift stores relieve the family of all the yelling. I can deal with my mother's criticisms of my outfits, but not the fighting. I try to tell that to my sisters, but they say they wouldn't be caught dead wearing somebody else's throwaways. What if the person died in them? What if they were wearing them the night of their murder?

Give me a break, I tell them.

And those two girls love to shop! Right off the rack! They never even look at the price tag; never even go to the clearance aisle. If it looks cute, they hand it to my mother who never says no. And we're not rich. Then she says in this kind of whiny voice, "See Hannah, if you like something, I'll be happy to get it for you. You know I will." It makes me so mad. Even if I like something in one of her stores, I'll never admit it to her. And now I'm used to buying stuff at thrift shops. And I really do love shopping there. I feel like I'm helping the planet. I'm glad people give their old stuff away. It's better than throwing it out! I wonder if people ever consider where their stuff goes after they throw it out? As if it's nice and tidy in their garbage can and just disappears! As if! So, I'd rather wear something that someone else wore than have it thrown away.

I also wonder who wore what I'm buying. What's their story? Did they get so fat they had to get rid of this great skirt or are they so rich they never even wore it? Will someone see me on the street and recognize that the shirt I'm wearing was once theirs? Occasionally I buy really old stuff, called vintage. The kind that really gives my sisters the creeps. Maybe someone actually did die while they were wearing it.

I believe in reincarnation. We talked about it in Riz's class. No one believed it but me. I thought it was such a far out concept. That you got a second, third or even fiftieth chance to get it right. When he was telling us about it, I thought I must have been really bad in a past life and that's why I wound up at this school.

At the thrift shop, I wonder if I'm buying clothes I might

have worn when I was somebody else. Buying my own clothes back. I'd never say these thoughts out loud, though. People already think I'm weird.

When I was three years old my parents took me to Chinatown in New York City. When it was time to go my father had to carry me kicking and screaming to the car. I couldn't leave, wouldn't leave. "I'm Chinese!" I screamed. "I live here!" My parents thought I was nuts, but I remember the feeling I had. Being in Chinatown felt so right , so normal, like I belonged there. And I was so young. It sounds like a past life memory if ever I heard one.

So, I go to the thrift shop some Saturdays or after school. The ladies who work there know me by now. They always let me know when the 'Fill a bag for a buck' days are going to happen. That's when I can really get good stuff. It totally annoys my mother. She rolls her eyes at me when I come into the house with my bag of old clothes. But hey, if I can find something that looks good, why not? The other day I got the grooviest pair of leather shoes. I think they're Earth Shoes, but they're so worn out, I can't tell the brand.

No matter what my mother says, I'll probably never shop in a department store again. My parents don't fight over anything but money, so if I don't spend any, they've got nothing to fight about! I've got to work on my sisters!

Doesn't my mother get it that I'm probably helping to save her marriage?

Chapter 27

"Don't you dare tell Mom what I did, she'll kill me!" I tell this to both my sisters. I meet them at Rader's, the candy store near Joni's school, where she's in third grade. Ruthie meets us there and after we buy our Starbursts, we start walking the eight blocks home.

We're all walking down the street and this car passes us and throws a lit cigarette butt right out onto the sidewalk where we're walking and I already mentioned how I feel about those. It almost hits Joni. I know I told my mother I'd stop doing this, but I can't help it this time. I run after the car, screaming for it to stop. I've done this before, lots of times, mostly to litterbugs, but this time I'm even madder, because it could've hurt my sister. The car pulls over and Ruthie and Joni are begging me not to go over to it, but I am fuming now and ready for anything.

The guy gets out, looking mean, but I'm ready for him. He thinks he's tough, the greaser. "Whadya want from me?" he says. Really bright.

"You threw your lit cigarette out the window and it nearly hit my sister. I'd like you to pick it up and apologize to her." I am standing in front of him, arms folded across my chest. I'm not scared, but my heart is pounding. He laughs and says I'm crazy, but then I take my notebook out of my book bag and start to write down his license plate number.

"Whadya think you're doing?"

"I'm going to report you to the police. There are fines for littering in this town, didn't you know? You could've started a fire, let alone burn my little sister." I can tell he's getting nervous. He's probably on probation or something. He's twitching now and I'm enjoying his discomfort. "The cigarette butt is right over there," I say, pointing to it. We see it, still smoldering, its ember glowing faintly on the grass. He seriously doesn't want to pick it up.

"Which model Chevy is it?" I ask, innocently.

He glares at me but walks over to the butt and picks it up, puts it out on the grass and sticks it into his jeans pocket. He mumbles, "Sorry," as he passes my sisters and gets back into the car and pulls away pretty fast. I am triumphant! Ruthie and Joni come up to me. I think they're going to congratulate me. Ruthie starts to cry and then Joni joins in.

"I can't believe you, Hannah. What is wrong with you?" Ruthie is glaring daggers at me. And then she punches me!

"That was so stupid! I hate you!" Even my little Joni is blaming me!

"I did it for you! He could've hurt you. And anyway, he

was polluting."

"I am going to tell Mom. I don't care what you say. Next time somebody's gonna get hurt, Hannah. You think you can just do that, to whoever you want?" Ruthie doesn't normally talk to me like this and I'm actually surprised and feeling a little guilty. Maybe she's right. Maybe that guy could've attacked us, or killed us or worse. Now I feel sick. I've done this kind of thing so many times before. I've always felt like some kind of Earth Avenger, trying to protect the planet from polluting jerks.

Once I saw a cop writing a ticket, then crumple up the carbon paper and drop it right on the street. I couldn't believe it and boy was I pissed! I rolled down the window to tell him off, but I was in the car with my mother who told me I'd better not. So I asked my dad who to write to and I wrote a letter to the Commissioner of Public Safety, telling him what I'd witnessed. A couple of months later, my father told me that the Commissioner, who happened to be a friend of his, had gotten my letter and the city actually changed to a carbonless ticket system! Because of me!

I haven't really ever given a thought to what I do. I just do it. I get so angry at people who pollute that I have to say something. I've come home out of breath before. Sometimes cars I stop chase me down. But I never really thought about Joni or Ruthie the way I do right now. As if their safety comes first.

"Please don't tell Mom. I promise not to do it again."

"Ever?" Joni asks me, expecting the truth.

"Not when you're around, at least."

"That's not good enough, Hannah. Don't do it, not when

you're alone or when you're with us!"

"Hannah! Promise or I will tell Mom. I mean it!" Ruthie is getting red in the face and I know she means it.

"All right, all right." I'm writhing inside. I try to keep my promises, I really do, but this one might be impossible. If I see someone throwing garbage out the window, how can I not say anything? How can I keep quiet and let them get away with it? Ruthie and Joni are looking at me like they don't believe me. They look so suspicious, it's almost funny. I smile at them and tell them to mellow out. I really will stop. Really. Really!

Chapter 28

Today was about the weirdest day I've ever had. It all started because of something that happened last week. Ruthie invited this new girl over to our house, Jill something or other. She was from the not-so-nice part of town and had never been to our neighborhood before. Of course this doesn't matter to us, where anyone's from. My mother is always encouraging us to make friends of all sorts (especially me). Jill seemed a bit weird, though. She kept commenting on our stuff and how nice everything was in the house. She kept looking around. I was a bit suspicious and watched her for a while before heading up to my room to listen to my new Dan Fogelberg album.

When I came downstairs for dinner, she was still over. I didn't really think anything about it. We always have people staying over for dinner. My mother hates for our friends to go home. Being an only child, a "lonely child" as she calls it, she probably wanted tons more kids. Amy used to be over for dinner at least three times a week. She loved my mother's cooking. She loved my mother, even more than her own, which made me jealous sometimes. She used to ask me if she could live with us. Of course I'd say sure, because I knew it'd never happen, but I never really wanted her to. My mom is mine. I've always felt that way and it's probably seriously immature, but I still do.

At about eight o'clock, Jill's mother comes to pick her up. Kelzee, our Keeshond, barks for a moment, and then spins around, chasing his tail. The woman is smoking a cigarette when she comes in, and I give my mother 'the look,' but she gives me one right back which says 'mind your own business.' My mother invites this stranger in and before you know it the two of them are deep in conversation and the woman is being invited for coffee. Luckily she left the rest of her cigarettes in the car.

Well, today when I get home from school, nobody is at home, which is kind of strange, and of course the doors are all unlocked, which I hate. I have tried to get my parents to lock the house, but they just laugh at me. Ever since we moved here from Queens, they think it's the country or something. Don't they watch the news? I mean, the reason we left Queens in the first place is enough to make anyone lock their doors and stay inside all the time.

It's because of me actually. I was six years old and playing alone in the courtyard of our garden apartment complex, waiting for my friend to come out and play. I guess my parents thought nothing of letting their six-year-old kid out alone in Queens! Anyway, this guy comes up to me and he just stands in front of me. He's wearing a trench coat and he doesn't say a word, just opens his coat and shows me everything. I mean everything! Then he closes his coat and leaves. I stand there for a while, stunned, then my friend comes out and we play. Later that night I mention the incident to my parents. I think we moved the next day.

Anyway, I guess my mother picked up Ruthie and Joni and they're shopping or something. I notice that something smells strange, like burnt toast and cigarette smoke, but nobody in the house smokes. Kelzee doesn't seem to be upset, so I just go into the kitchen to have a snack. There is something smoldering in the toaster! I unplug the thing and pull out what looks like a piece of dishtowel. Now I'm scared. I grab a big umbrella out of the closet to use as a weapon and I check the downstairs. It's clear. Then I head upstairs slowly. I mean, what the hell is going on? It really stinks like cigarettes up here. I'm trying not to freak out and I wonder if the windows are open and old Mrs. Lange from next door is having a smoke fest.

The smell is coming from the bathroom. I can tell you that my heart is pounding as I push open the door. The toilet seat is down, which is pretty unusual. No one in this family ever puts it down. I lift it up and almost barf. The bowl is full of burned out cigarette butts. I despise cigarettes, hate them, but seeing them this way totally grosses me out and I'm not sure what to do. I flush the toilet, but there are so many of them in there that the toilet starts to overflow! Oh, God, I'm gonna be sick.

Where is everybody! I'd better call Dad at his office! I run into their room to use the phone, and there in my parent's bed, wearing my mother's fluffy light blue bathrobe is Jill's mother, passed out. My heart is pounding and I'm freaking out. Totally freaking out. Panic. Oh God!

I check to see if she's breathing and then I notice something. A prescription bottle on the bed. It has her name on it, and it's empty. Oh, great, just great! She's dead on my parents' bed! No, she's alive! She's turning and groaning. Help!

I'm shaking as I dial my father's office. His secretary answers and I tell her I need to speak to him. It's an emergency. I can hear the exasperation in his voice when he comes on, like he thinks whatever the reason is I'm calling, could not possibly be an emergency. He's very busy.

"Dad, you've got to come home, NOW!"

"Hannah, what is it? What's wrong?"

"Dad, there is a woman in your bed, wearing Mom's robe!"

"Hannah, where's your mother?"

"I DON'T KNOW! Just come home!"

"Hannah, calm down and explain the situation to me." He hears me hyperventilating now, which I am. I hear the door slam. Oh, thank God. I hear my mother call up the stairs.

"Is that your mother? Hannah, Hannah?" I don't even answer him. I just throw the phone down on the bed and run downstairs, three at a time. I am gripping my chest as I run into the kitchen. She hears me flying down the stairs and her back is to me, she's sniffing. "What is that smell, Hannah?" I know she doesn't think I've been smoking. She turns around, sees my face. "Hannah? What's the matter?"

My sisters see my face too and Ruthie goes, "What's wrong? Hannah!"

I just point up the stairs. I really don't want to go back up there.

Now my mother looks scared. "Hannah, what is going on?"

"Just come up. Hurry!" I gasp.

"Hannah!" I can tell she doesn't want to follow me, but of course she does. I turn around and see my two sisters following and I yell for them to stay where they are. They both start to whine, but they stay put.

"Hannah, you're scaring me."

"Yeah, well, how do you think I feel?"

I lead her into the bedroom and she stands there at the doorway, flabbergasted. Jill's mother is starting to move around, groaning. Then she throws up. Right on my mother's bed. I start to gag.

"Hannah, call the police." I just stand there, gagging.

"Hannah! DO it!"

I run downstairs; I just can't stay in that room. I pick up the phone, but it's doing that crazy beeping thing when someone leaves it off the hook. I scream to my mother to hang it up. Then I call the cops and tell them what happened and to come right over. I give them the address. My sisters are standing next to me, their eyes bulging out of their heads. They start to carry on.

"Hannah! I'm scared! What's going on?"

"Oh, my God, is somebody dead up there? Hannah?!"

"Shut up! Shut up!" I am not sympathetic at all. Then I realize that I probably scared the daylights out of them. "Don't worry," I say, trying to gentle the tone of my voice. "It's okay now. Mom is taking care of it and the police are coming." Oh, yeah, that really helps. They start screaming even louder.

My father, whose office is only a few blocks away, bursts into the house, gives us all a look and rushes up the stairs. We can hear him yelling at mom. "I tell you time and again, not to be so damn friendly to everybody…"

I can just picture him, sitting on the edge of the puke covered bed, shaking that head of his.

My mother can't help it. She takes in stray people. But that's what makes her so loveable and Dad knows it. He's not really mad and when I go back upstairs, he's holding her tightly next to him. She looks down at Jill's mother and her face is extremely sad. She looks at her with such pity that I'm less angry at this strange woman who has broken into our house.

The police are knocking. Thank God my father is here. He takes over and I just watch from the doorway as they get her up and try to talk to her. She's pretty incoherent. I hear sirens and then the paramedics come bounding up the stairs. She is still wearing my mother's robe, as they carry her out on a stretcher. I think my father bought it for her.

The cop asks me a ton of questions and I feel like I'm being interrogated. Except that he's being very gentle, because he can see how freaked out I still am. My father is upstairs working on cleaning out the toilet. I think it'll be a long time before I want to use that bathroom. I'll use the small one, even though I hate it. It's right next to the basement stairs.

The police leave and my mother goes upstairs and changes her sheets. How she's going to sleep in that bed again is a mystery to me. Thank the Lord that woman didn't climb into mine!

But I think Ruthie is the most upset. It's her friend's mother after all. I know she's feeling guilty that she brought that woman into our house, but nobody is blaming her. It wasn't her fault.

My mother is calling Jill to see if anyone else is home at her house. Yes, her grandmother lives with them. Her parents are divorced. My mother is speaking with the grandmother, telling her what's happened. She's being so nice! What is this? I mean, for God's sake, the woman broke into our house (okay, let herself in), tried to kill herself and stole my mother's bathrobe!

I watch my mother on the phone, first reassuring, then listening to the grandmother. She is nodding her head, saying yes, and oh, that's too bad and oh, I had no idea… She is a very good listener. My father sometimes tells her she should charge people for it. But that's probably why that woman came here to have her episode. She probably felt safe.

She hangs up the phone and comes over to me. She puts her arms around me and hugs me very tightly. I hug her back and start to cry. I want to be little again. I want her to rub my back like she used to.

We go out for dinner, leaving all the windows open to air out the smell of vomit and cigarettes. No one wants to stay home. And my mother locks the doors.

It's hard for any of us to sleep. I toss and turn for what feels like hours. I fall asleep to the sound of Ruthie snoring from her room and my parents quietly talking, the TV on low. I dream about my mother taking in dozens of stray cats.

Chapter 29

"Hannah, telephone!" Mom is calling me from downstairs. How come nobody in this family can just come up and tell you something?

"Who is it?" I yell back.

"Andy? I think he said his name was Andy."

Oh, God. My heart which was calmly beating, listening to John Denver, begins to pound, rapid fire. It's pounding in my ears and I think I'm going deaf.

"Hannah, he's waiting!"

I feel like I'm in slow motion as I walk to her bedroom where the other phone sits by her bed. The phone looks shaky to me and strange. I pick it up and say, "Got it, Mom." I wait until I hear her hang up and then I say, "Hello?" really quietly.

"Hannah? Is that you?"

"Uh huh." God, do I sound stupid.

"It's Andy, from Three Rivers, do you remember me?"

Is he kidding? Remember him? I was (am) completely and totally in love with him. We met this past summer at a wilderness camp in Vermont. We were both counselors there. He was the most gorgeous boy I had ever seen. Exactly my type. Perfect for me. I tried to flirt with him in my pathetic way. When the camp took its annual trip out west and we were given a choice of where we wanted to hike, I chose to climb the glacier at Lake Louise. Not because I actually wanted to strap into ropes and wear crampons and climb a freezing glacier in the middle of August, and fall in a crevasse, which I did. No, I chose it because Andy did. I was the only girl out there on the ice. I thought maybe I'd have a chance with him, maybe he'd see me as his perfect woman, the kind of girl he'd been waiting for his whole life. But I was just one of the guys.

We used to give each other backrubs. Nothing too sexy, but nice. We all did it, and it was pretty innocent. I gave him a really good one, one night back at camp, in his cabin. We were all sitting around rubbing each other's backs. He seemed to be enjoying it. I know I was. A few days later, just before camp ended, we were all talking about who gave the best massages. Andy sat there, in front of me and said, "You know who gives the best massages?" I smiled, blushed, sure he was going to say I did. He said, "Merelda does, God is she amazing!"

I was glad the cabin was lit only by candles. I don't think anyone saw what happened to my face or my heart. I thought that if I looked at myself just then, I would have seen angry welts all over my face and body, like I got once when I swam unknowingly into a school of nasty jellyfish.

Merelda! I couldn't believe it. Self-named Merelda was also a self-proclaimed witch. She told everyone she practiced black magic. Described the sacrifices she said she had participated in. And I believed her. She used to have the most horrible and incredibly loud nightmares. She'd wake us all up with her screaming and cursing. But oh yes, what a massage she gave! Yipdeedoo. Her name was actually Marsha, a Jewish girl from Long Island. I'm sure she took her lame witchy name from Esmerelda, one of Samantha's witch relatives on "Bewitched!" I found her mean and tragic, but I guess Andy found her something else.

"Of course I remember you. How are you?" I think I'm stuttering. I can hardly hear myself through all the hammering that's going on.

"I'm great. I'm coming home from SUNY Cobleskill for a break this week and I told Tim I'd visit, and I thought maybe we could all get together."

Why does he want to get together? To torture me? To make me suffer?

"I'd love to get together. When would you be coming?" I think I am going to die. I need to throw up. I wish he'd finish this conversation.

"I was hoping to stop by this Saturday. Then we could go together to visit Tim."

Tim is a great guy, another counselor who lives about 45 minutes from here in a ritzy town in Connecticut in what I would call a mansion. I visited him once after my first year at camp. We call him Doc. He wants to be like Reinhold Messner, the greatest climber in the world.

"Sure, that'd be great."

"Excellent! Can you give me directions?"

This I can do. This is technical and boring. Roads and streets. Not hearts or feelings. My directions are perfect.

"See you Saturday, Hannah!" he says and it sounds like he's smiling. Do I have a chance? Dare I dream?

Chapter 30

Saturday cannot come too soon and I wish it would never come at all. The thought of seeing Andy is too much for me. The thought that he's going to come to my house, be up in my room, makes me sick with terror and anticipation at the same time. What is he thinking? Did he finally realize that I am the one for him, not Merelda/Marsha? Will he confess his love for me? Should I tell him how I feel? Not first of course, but after he tells me?

I can't concentrate. Mr. O'Brien is moving his mouth, lecturing about the Mississippi River, but I can't hear a word he's saying. I need to get out of this building. I raise my hand and ask to go to the girl's room. He nods and I leave quickly. I cannot breathe properly and it's only Wednesday. I can't wait until Sunday, when it's all over and I can either revel in the sheer beauty of what happened on Saturday or lick the wounds I endured. I feel pathetic.

In the metal mirror in the bathroom, I look distorted. Is that really how I look? I pull my fingers through my hair and slowly walk back to class. The "Be Good" lady is there, standing in her place in the hall. "Be good!" she tells me as I walk by.

"Oh, yes. I will," I tell her. Am I ever anything but?

Saturday comes racing in like a marathon runner, and I'm as breathless as one. I am wearing the same Indian blouse I wore on that fateful day at the bleachers. I am not superstitious. The shirt is pretty and it looks good on me. I made Andy a macramé bracelet. Very masculine, with thick string and smooth wooden beads. I am waiting in my room, pacing the floors when I hear a car pull up. Kelzee starts to bark. I look out and see a Land Rover in front of the house. A Land Rover! Oh, he is so my type. And there he is, his long hair, his broad shoulders. He's wearing a woolen jacket with a scarf and hiking boots. What will I do if this is just a friendly visit? I am gulping for breath. I need oxygen! Calm down, Hannah. I try to steady myself. This is sick! He's just a person, like anyone else. The doorbell rings. Kelzee is barking and twirling around. I open the door and smile, probably too broadly. But he's smiling too. Is that a good sign?

"Hannah."

"Hi, Andy."

"Hi." He is waiting for something, but my mind is going blank. Then I notice the steam coming out of his mouth as he breathes.

"Oh, come in!" What a jerk. Let the guy in! It's 20 degrees out there.

"Thanks." He comes in and waves at something behind me. I turn and see my mother and two sisters peering out from the kitchen. They are smiling and waving stupidly. I give them the look and they disappear back into the lemony room.

"Let's go upstairs." I lead the way. C'mon Hannah, I tell myself, you're almost seventeen. You can do this. You can make him love you.

"Neat room! I remember this." He is holding my remembrance stick. Everyone at camp made one. Just a stick with everyone's autograph on it. Some people drew little pictures on it. Andy signed mine. It is a large Maple bough with a burl in the middle of it. I polished it until it shone and then let everyone sign it.

"Look at what Merelda drew!" He is smiling at the horrid little drawing, a little demonic face, the only thing on the stick that taints it. I tried not to let her sign it, but we were all there, gathered in the mess hall. It would have been too obvious.

"Yeah, cute," I say, lamely.

"I heard from her, you know. She's doing much better. She left her coven."

Don't talk about her! I was hoping she'd be burned at the stake.

"Wow, that's great. Whatever she was into was way too negative. She was really spooky with those nightmares, don't you think?"

He doesn't think so. He just smiles and says, "You just didn't get to know her."

Could you leave? Are we going to spend my dream Saturday discussing the wicked witch of wilderness camp? I hand him the gift I made him. It is rolled in a piece of birch bark, tied in a strip of leather.

"I made this for you." He takes it and gives me a long considering look. I squirm under it but I am not going to look away. He opens it carefully, not ripping the soft fabric of the bark. He exclaims when he sees what I have made. I look at him to see if he's being sarcastic. He's not.

"Put it on me." He extends his arm to me and when I place the bracelet around it, touching his wrist slightly, I'm shaking so hard I can barely get the thing hooked. He looks at it, admiring it.

"You made this?" Does he really not know me at all?

"Andy, I was the arts and crafts counselor, remember? Just give me some string and I can make anything."

"Yeah." We don't talk about Merelda anymore, thank you, Lord. He walks around my room admiring the photos I have tacked up on my walls. "Did you take these?" he asks, surprised.

"Yes." I wish he didn't sound so astonished.

"These are great! You should consider majoring in photography. Where do you want to go school anyway?"

We talk about college and his experiences there and then there's this awkward silence. He has brought his cross country skis and seeing that there's snow on the ground, he'd like to go. Is there anywhere we can ski nearby? I tell him we can go to the golf course a few miles away. I am imagining him kissing me on the white greenway.

We get there and someone has already made tracks. Probably my father, who skis to his office every time it snows, even a few inches. We ski around for an hour or so until it becomes boring, going round and round the golf course. We climb back into his Land Rover and leave for Tim's. I'll go anywhere, just as long as I can stay with him. He seems to know where he's going. We talk about his college. He's in his first year, studying forestry. I tell him about high school, Riz, my "D" paper, but not much else. Not my lack of friends, not my therapist. Definitely not my loneliness. Maybe today will change all that. That's what I keep wishing, all day.

Tim is expecting us and he looks so different from when I saw him last. Last time I saw him, he was wearing rip-stop pants, rock climbing shoes, and a tee shirt that said "Go climb a rock!" Now he's dressed in tan pleated pants and loafers, with tassels! His mother is wearing a bow tie on a frilly blouse. She is serving us cocoa on a silver tray. We sit on her white sofa and smile, thanking her, hoping like hell that she'll leave the room. Tim looks at us with what I can only imagine is sheer desperation. Andy and I nod in acknowledgement. I feel like I'm part of something subversive and sneaky. She means well, but really, a bow tie! She finally takes her leave, inviting us to eat the sugar cookies she's made.

"Thanks, Mom," Tim says a little too sharply. He rolls his eyes at us and whispers, "I've got to get back to school! I'm suffocating here!"

"I hear you, man," Andy says, sympathetically. Does his mother wear a bow tie too?

It's weird, being together this way. Tim looks so uncomfortable and out of place in his own house. I feel sorry for him. If I'd known it would be like this, I wouldn't have let Andy bring me. I think about taking pictures, but I don't. I want to picture Doc like I've always seen him. Hanging upside down from the rafters of the mess hall lodge, his long blonde hair pulled back with a strip of leather. Or rappelling down a rock face, calling out, "On Belay! Belay on!"

We don't stay too long, which is fine with me. I think we all are feeling strange. It's never the same, these reunions. We can't recreate our friendships in the outside world, the non-camp world. They are too unique and special. Something for summers only. Magical days, free from parents and school and responsibilities, where you can be whoever you think you really are, not who you're supposed to be. I guess that's when I know that nothing is going to happen between me and Andy. He is my camp love and I am his good friend. Maybe we'll see each other next summer at camp, if we both return. He might have an internship out west. Yeah, and I might be sailing around the world.

He drives me home and he gives me the sweetest kiss I have ever had. I admit it, it's my first. Yeah, I know. Sweet sixteen and never been kissed. But it was nice. Not one of those Hollywood kisses, but so nice. He says goodbye, that he'll call me or write, but I know he never will and my insides twist with longing and embarrassment. Does he have any idea how I feel? He will be in my dreams for a long time, I know. After he leaves I go up to my room and put on James's album "Gorilla" and play "I was a Fool to Care" over and over again.

I hope he'll wear the bracelet until it falls off.

Chapter 31

I wake up on my birthday to Mom kissing my cheek and Dad singing the birthday song in his deep voice. My sisters, hearing the fanfare from their room next door, run into my room and jump onto my bed.

"Happy Birthday!" Joni shrieks. Ruthie joins in with Dad, forcing her voice into a Louie Armstrong rendition. I have to smile.

"Poppy and Helen are coming over tonight with their gift for you," my mother says, an air of mystery in her voice.

"What's he gonna give her? A box of Cracker Jacks?"

"Ruthie, that's terrible!" my mother scolds.

"Yeah, maybe there'll be a great toy surprise!" Joni adds, never wanting to be left out.

"Girls! That's enough! You know very well that it's the thought that counts." My mother is trying to sound convincing. She knows they're right. She knows how cheap her father is. But maybe he will come through for me this year. I think my mother wants this birthday to be great, even more than I do.

I know Mom is worried about me. I can see it in the sad way she looks at me. She feels guilty, as if she's done something wrong. As if it's her fault I am so unhappy. I moped around the house for three weeks after my outing with Andy. And no, I haven't gotten a call or a letter yet.

She tried to bad-mouth him, maybe to make me feel better, or maybe she was angry that he doesn't love me, but I love him no matter what, even if he never calls me again. Even if the visit was out of pity. I told her not to talk meanly about him. We are friends, I tell her. Just good friends. I tell myself the same thing. One more to add to my list of one.

My mother was painfully shy as a child, almost phobic. But she had friends. She knows what happened with Amy and the others and I think she blames herself somehow. She wanted me to go to the parties, even though she knew what went on there. But to her, friends are more important than anything. She was an only child and really knew the meaning of loneliness. She begged her parents to have another kid. But her father had been too busy being a soldier, an army dentist, re-enlisting twice during the war.

Of course she's glad that I don't take drugs, but even she thinks I'm an oddball.

I doubt anyone at school will remember it's my birthday, not even Amy. She didn't last year, or if she did, she didn't acknowledge it. We used to talk about our birthdays for weeks before they came. We memorized each other's and would always buy each other gifts at our favorite store, Rainbow's End.

May 12. That was hers. It still is, I suppose. But this year, this day, no one pays any attention to me. That's okay. I don't need anything from anyone.

I wonder what my parents are going to give me.

I go through the school day like I have some terrible secret, but no one wants to know it. But it's my birthday and it's important to me. At lunch I tell Richard.

"Hannah, why didn't you tell me it was coming? I would've done something!"

"That's okay, Richard, I don't need a thing." Liar!

"Hannah, what is your problem anyway!" Richard says, smiling. He appreciates my weirdness. Maybe he'll give me something tomorrow. That would be nice.

Six o'clock. Poppy and Helen arrive in their huge white Dodge. They pull into the driveway and honk the horn, as usual. We all come running out of the house. Why we always run when they come over is beyond me, we know what awaits us. Slobbery kisses and scratches from Poppy's stubbly, saggy face.

"Hellllooo!" he says, grabbing each of us one at a time. We try not to make it too obvious, the wiping off of his kisses with our sleeves.

"Hello, dahlings!" Helen cries. She is such a ham! We know she used to be an actress. She wiggles around on her spike heels giving us all faux kisses. Tonight she is wearing furry pompoms on the tips of her shoes. Her feet must be freezing, but I guess being sexy is more important than frostbite.

"Daddy! Helen!" Mom comes out the kitchen door and Poppy grabs her in a tight hug. He's whispering something to her and she's glancing over at the car. Oh, please God. It's not so bad, I tell myself. It's a nice car.

We all go inside and Helen stays in the kitchen with Mom. Poppy sits on the green sofa in the living room and pulls Joni onto his lap.

"Look what I brought you, you little monkey!" He reaches inside his jacket pocket and pulls out a fake gold ring with a big fake red jewel.

"Thanks, Poppy!" Joni says. She is smirking behind his back as she hugs him. This makes about twenty nine in her collection. Ruthie and I stifle a laugh.

"Hey what about me!" Ruthie cries, in mock distress. She's as bad as Helen.

"Come over here!" Joni jumps down, happy I'm sure to get off Poppy's lap and makes room for Ruthie. Ruthie sits next to the old man. I mean, she's almost thirteen. He pulls something out of another pocket and hands it to her. It's a little better than what he gave Joni, but not much. It's a magnifying glass that seems to work, somewhat.

"Thanks, Poppy," Ruthie says, rolling her eyes at us.

"Hannah, I've got your present outside. When we're ready to go, I'll give it to you. Okay?"

"Sure, Poppy. That's fine," I say this calmly, but my heart is pounding at the thought of the old white Dodge. They must have bought something else. Helen can't drive, so they only need one car. I wonder how they'll plan on presenting it to me, if it really is the car.

"Let's get going!" Mom calls from the kitchen. I grab my

grandfather's rough hand and pull him off the couch.

"Not so fast, Hannah. This old man ain't what he used to be."

"That's not true, my dahling!" Helen appears, slurring somewhat, tumbler in hand, empty except for a few melting ice cubes.

She grabs him tightly around the waist, causing the three of us to heave inwardly, their displays of affection always so revolting.

"C'mon, Milt, let's give our beautiful, yet ever so skinny grandchild her birthday present." She catches my hand and lovingly squeezes it. I can't help loving this eccentric old bird. It took me a while to accept her, after Nanny died, but she's really amusing. She's got a million stories and she makes us laugh. And Poppy is incredibly happy.

"Yes, let's go," I agree and briskly guide them back to their coats and then to the driveway.

We stand around the car, our breath coming out like clouds, waiting expectantly. Poppy, with a flourish, as if performing a magic act with Helen as his assistant, sweeps his arm toward his wife. She bows and opens her purse as if it were a magic box. From inside her clutch, she dramatically pulls out a package wrapped in shiny paper. She hands it to Poppy who moves to stand in front of me, his oldest grandchild.

"For you, my Hannah Banana on her 17th birthday," he says seriously. "Use it in good health. Mazel Tov!"

My hands are shaking as I slowly open the present. Ruthie and Joni are jumping up and down telling me to hurry up. My mother is leaning against the side of the house with a satisfied smile. I wish my father was here to see this, but he's meeting us at the restaurant.

Inside the box is a key on a plastic key chain. I look closely at it and my heart leaps. It has the Dodge insignia.

"Oh, my God! Poppy, Helen! Thank you!"

"What is it?" my sisters are nearly hysterical with anticipation.

"Can I show them? I mean really show them?" I ask.

Poppy and Helen nod and I unlock the car door and climb in. My car is white with red interior and has one of those skinny steering wheels with a skinny bar of a horn. It has an AM radio and not much else, but it's mine! Poppy and Helen bought themselves another used car, much newer than my '68 Dodge; a 1973 Buick Regal, sky blue. It'll match one of Helen's negligees.

I tell my sisters to get in. They look over at Mom for permission and she nods. We're all grinning stupidly as I start up the engine. My own car! I can't believe it! My grandfather finally came through! Everyone squeezes in and Mom lets me drive us all to Szechuan Royal, sitting next to me in the front seat, putting her feet on imaginary brakes and gasping every now and then.

Chapter 32

I have to baby-sit for my sisters tonight. My parents are going to some political dinner where they're going to honor my father. My mother is wearing a gown and has her hair done up in twists and curls, and she looks nothing like herself. My father is wearing a tuxedo and he put hairspray on. My mother is forever trying to make his crazy Beethoven-like hair stay down. I can tell she's happy tonight, because his hair is flat on his head. I think he looks weird.

I despise baby-sitting. Especially here. I don't mind it at neighbors' houses, where they pay me and where they have security systems. But all we have is Kelzee, who lets strange women into the house. If another intruder comes, I'll be the one who has to protect my sisters and myself.

My father hands me the red-marked TV guide, pointing to what we are allowed to watch. My father calls everything that isn't educational, 'drivel' or 'swill' and red-marks the TV guide, allowing us to watch only what is on his list. My mother whispers on her way out, "Watch whatever you want to and get them to bed by ten. We won't be too late." She kisses me on the cheek and follows Dad out. I lock all the doors; bolt them, chain them and put chairs in front of them. There are three. (I was pretty bad before the blue bathrobe incident, as we call it, but I'm way worse now.) Then I open the basement door, peering into the gloom and think about whether or not to go down there and make sure the hatch is fastened. That basement is like a house of horrors. It's damp and dark, even with the one bulb hanging in the laundry room. I cannot believe my mother can do our laundry down there. Doesn't she get the creeps? When my dad bought me my enlarger he actually wanted me to set up my darkroom down there! Nope, I told him. The downstairs bathroom has no windows and would do just fine, thank you.

There's a wine cellar behind a tiny door, almost like a crawl space. The people who owned this house before us kept wine, but we don't have anything in there, which makes it creepier. If it had some purpose, it might not be so frightening.

There's a broken rocking horse and a deep freezer. I watched a movie once where this woman kills her husband with a frozen turkey leg and then drags him down to the basement and puts him in the freezer. When the cops come to investigate, she serves them the turkey. They eat the evidence.

"Hannah, what are you doing?" I almost have a heart attack. Ruthie is breathing down my neck.

"What do you think I'm doing?"

"Just shut the door and let's watch Nancy Drew."

"No, we'd better go down and check the hatch."

"Who cares? I think it's already locked."

"Well, I don't. Come with me."

"Give me a break. I'm going up to watch my show. Come if you want."

There's a sound from under the stairs. We look at each other.

"Where's Irving?" Irving is our cat, who we thought was a male, but then he gave birth on Ruthie's bed at three o'clock one morning. We realized we'd made a mistake.

"I don't know. That was probably her. Hannah, I'm going upstairs."

"Fine, be that way. If someone breaks in, again, don't blame me."

She gives me a withering look and says, "Then go and lock it. I'll wait right here."

Sometimes I'm ashamed of these fears. Especially because neither of my sisters cares if any doors are locked when my parents aren't here. I know they think I'm a freak. I walk down the creaky wooden stairs and pull the string for the bulb near the hatch. I see Ruthie's right. It is locked. I pick up an old mop to use as a weapon and look around to make sure there's no one there. Irving jumps off the dryer and runs up the stairs, causing my heart to leap. I clutch my hand to my chest then quickly pull the light string and run like hell up the stairs. I practically shove Ruthie out of the way to get out of there. She looks at me as if I'm seriously bizarre and trudges up the stairs. I shut the door and pull the small deadbolt across it, breathing hard.

I go into the kitchen and stand against the refrigerator for a moment, catching my breath, then serve three bowls of ice cream and bring them upstairs. Joni and Ruthie haven't a care in the world as they lie on our parents' bed (the infamous bed, I call it) and watch their show. They love it when I baby-sit. We watch anything we want to, red mark or no, and I stay with them. I don't go into my room or hang out by myself. Not when my parents aren't home. And I don't know why they like it when I stay with them, because they don't normally seem to like me much.

We watch The Nancy Drew Mysteries and then a couple of other shows. I dread the fact that it's ten o'clock. I don't want them to go to bed. That means I'll be alone. So I let them stay up until nearly eleven, but Joni's falling asleep on the big bed. I wake her up, make her brush her teeth, and then throw her into her own bed. Ruthie follows her and then I am alone. My parents still aren't home. The clock on my father's side of the bed says 11:47. Saturday Night Live is already on. Gilda Radner is doing a skit where she is a child and her parents put her to bed. She gets up to look in the closet and there is a disgusting monster in it. She's screaming and when her parents run in to check, of course there's nothing there.

I hear voices outside. I peer out the side of the curtains and see two men standing by a parked car. What the hell are they doing out there? Should I call the police? Oh, God. My mouth feels dry. I go downstairs and pull a knife out of the kitchen drawer, and then I fly back up the stairs and go back to my position by the window. I can still hear the men, but I can't see them. Oh, where are they?

Then I see two women coming out of my neighbor's

house and the two men come out of the shadows. Oh, no! Are they going to get raped right in front of my house? But no, the two men put their arms around their wives and walk them to their car. My breath is coming ragged and I feel dizzy. I look over to the TV and see Chevy Chase falling off his news anchor chair. I try to laugh, but a laugh is not what comes out of my mouth. I look out the window again. Nothing. Quiet. Suburbia.

By the time I hear my parents, I can tell my father is really ticked off. I hear his loud, harsh whisper. "Hannah! Hannah!" Then, tap, tap, tap on the window. Oh, my God, I've left them standing outside while I was asleep at my post! For how long? No one could get in with my security system.

I run downstairs and move the chair, unbolt and unlock the door. My father is shaking his head in his characteristic gesture. They smell like perfume and alcohol. My mother puts her hand on my cheek and whispers, "Sorry we're late."

We all go upstairs. I'm not even sure they bother to lock the back door. It takes me a long time to get to sleep and I lie awake listening to my parents' hushed conversation. I wonder if they're talking about me.

Chapter 33

The girls' room is packed as I try and wash my hands. Girls are pushing their way closer to the mirror putting on makeup. A couple of them are smoking in the stalls and I really want to leave, but I hear something that makes me take notice, and I stay even though I'll walk out smelling like an ashtray.

"....yeah, your brother is a freak."

"Yeah, and that's why he's going to the Project. No way could he make it in this school. So now he's gonna be with a bunch of geeks and retards. It's so embarrassing."

"It's got nothing to do with you..."

I want them to say more, but their makeup is on and they walk out. I stand there in the smoke filled haze, my mind reeling. Can't make it in this school? With a bunch of geeks? Not that I'm one, although I've often wondered if geeks and nerds know they're geeks and nerds. I don't think I'm one, but who knows? Or cares for that matter. What is the Project? Where is it? And why have I never heard of it before? Is it part of this school?

A girl comes out of the stall, a huge pink bubble sticking out of her mouth. It pops and smoke pours from it. I shoot out of there and storm into my guidance counselor's office. There is someone there but I stand there, my arms folded defiantly. I'll wait. I see her shift uncomfortably in her chair and I hear her say in a low voice, "Sherry, can we talk about this later?" The girl nods and looks over at me. She leaves and I remain standing.

"What's the Project?"

"Excuse me?" She's adjusting her glasses.

"I said, what is the Project?"

She clears her throat and looks shifty.

"Well?"

"Well Hannah, it's no place I've ever considered for you."

"I didn't ask you that. I asked you what it is. Could you tell me what it is?" I am not asking.

She is looking really uncomfortable and I don't care. "Well, it's an alternative school at the church down the road. It's actually called the Schoolhouse Option Project."

"Who's it for?" My voice is starting to get loud.

"It's for students who cannot get along in the mainstream high school."

At this point I sit down, hard, in the chair across from her. I can feel my eyes begin to bulge from my head as I glare at her.

"And why is it a place you never considered for me? Is it

just for derelicts? Morons? Retards?"

Now she sits straight up and tries to put on her firm but gentle attitude. I'm not buyin' it.

"No, Hannah, it is not. It's for those either too bright to get along here or too, um, dim. I didn't think you fit either category."

This reminds me of Mrs. Ruby, my first grade teacher, who separated me from my best friend, putting her in the "Smart" math group, and putting me in the "Stupid" math group. I swear to God it's true! She didn't even have the brains to call the groups "the Cheetahs" and "the Turtles" or whatever. I cried because I wanted to be with my friend. She told me not to cry, she was giving me the honored position of head of the "Stupid" group! No wonder I can't do math!

"No, Mrs. Schultz, I think you never consider what I need."

"Hannah, your grades are not up to par, nor are you in the category of, how shall I put it?"

"Uh, stupid, underachiever, dimwit?"

"Well..."

"I want to go and see for myself. Make me an appointment." I am ready to explode and I hope for her sake she's right.

"I don't think that's necessary. They're all full."

"Then I'm going to call my mother and she'll demand you make that appointment." If my mother knew I talked to my guidance counselor this way, she'd have such a fit. She's forever wanting to tape record my tone of voice so I can hear how nasty I sound. I already know.

"There's no need to get huffy with me, young lady. Even

if you like the school, there are no openings for this year. You'd have to wait until you're a senior." Why is she looking defiant and challenging? Isn't she a guidance counselor who has kids' best interests in mind? Isn't that her job? Guidance? I'm going to look up that word in the dictionary. As far as I'm concerned it means someone who guides and helps others. And she's my guidance counselor. She was assigned to me!

I wait in her office until she calls my mom for permission, which of course she gets, and then she calls the school and makes the appointment. They can see me the next day.

I drive myself in the morning. I'm going to spend the whole day. I'm greeted by a smiling woman who brings me into the common room. The school is in the basement of the Methodist church. They use the Sunday school classrooms. It's small and there are hardly any kids. They are all sitting in a circle. They're about to have some kind of morning meeting.

The woman introduces me and everyone says hi or waves. The teacher leading the group is called Rick. Rick! Not Mr. Whatever, but his real name!

"Welcome to the Project, Hannah."

"Thanks," I say. Kids are smiling at me, nodding. I think I recognize a couple of them from junior high.

"Hannah, every morning we talk about how the previous day went and how we want this day to go. And on Fridays we all talk about how the week went. Feel free to chime in anytime. We use the talking stick, so if you have something to say, just raise your hand and it will be passed to you."

This is so cool. They share stories and feelings and it is so incredible. I feel like crying. Rick asks me if I have anything to say. I do. Someone passes me the stick. I look at it for a moment. It reminds me of my memory stick from camp.

"Why didn't I know about this place before?"

Kids are nodding and talking at once. Rick puts up his hand and everyone stops. He hands the stick to a guy with glasses.

"No one told me either. I found out through a friend of a friend. I was as pissed off as I bet you are right now."

He passes the stick to a girl with really short pitch-black hair and three rings in each ear.

"It's not really a secret school, but no one at the high school ever talks about it. It's kind of taboo over there. They think we're all freaks. Anyway, it seems like you have to find out about it through word of mouth. I guess because there are hardly any spaces available. You really have to want to come here and maybe karmically, when you're ready, you'll find out about it."

It is so cool that she's talking about karma. Maybe Riz should work here instead. The meeting ends and I have tears in my eyes, which I quickly wipe away. I might have had friends if I was here. I might have actually liked school.

I am so angry at Mrs. Schultz that I'm ready to tear her apart. This school is perfect. For me, at least. I want to scream and have a tantrum. Three years wasted! Three years! Good thing I won't see her until tomorrow. I might do something I'll regret.

I stay for the whole day going to art class where they're doing ceramics, I go to Social Studies, where they're having an intense discussion about slavery and secession. Everyone participates and it's really interesting! I wish I could come here the next day and the rest of the year. I'm even more depressed now than ever, knowing what I might have had, knowing that I have to put in three more months at my internment camp.

At dinner, my parents want to know about my experience.

"So, how was the Project? Did you learn anything?" my father asks.

"Yes, and I'm going there next year!"

"Hold on, hold on. Hannah, your impulsivity is going to get you into trouble." He is shaking his head as he bites into his chicken cutlet. Why must the man be so negative? I like going on impulse, and anyway, he knows how much I hate high school.

"Dad, it was great! It's still part of the high school, just an alternative section." I'm trying to speak rationally. I know he thinks I'm too emotional, so I'm trying to tone it down.

"Were there nice kids?" Of course my mom wants to know this.

"Yeah, lots and I think I could be friends with some of them. They've got great courses and if I do well, I could still get into a good college." This is for my father who'd like me to go to Harvard like he did. Right! I want to threaten to drop out if they say no, but instead, I tell them about the classes and the morning meeting. They look at each other, raising their eyebrows, which means they will consider it, and by the end of the meal, they've agreed to let me enroll.

I storm Mrs. Schultz's office as soon as I get to school the next day. I don't even wait for her to swallow her coffee. I hope she burns her tongue.

"Enroll me."

"Excuse me?"

"You say that every time. I'm speaking plain English. I said, enroll me. My parents agreed."

"It is not as easy as that, Hannah. There are forms to fill out, waiting lists to get on."

"You call yourself a guidance counselor. Well, Mrs. Schultz, I actually looked up the word guidance. Here's what it said." I pull a piece of paper out of my pocket and read it aloud, "Guidance; the act or function of guiding, leadership; direction. Advice or counseling service for students. A program of care or assistance in the treatment of minor emotional disturbances. Something that guides." She is staring at me.

"When have you ever guided me? Advised me? I told you last year about Mr. Meandro. Did you even talk to him? Ask him to stop humiliating me? No, you advised me to grin and bear it!

"You know I hate to eat lunch in the cafeteria. Did you ever invite me to eat with you or find me a place I could feel comfortable? No, you advised me to just get out of the hall and get back into the cafeteria.

"And now, you've apparently known about this school all this time, all this time! After I've told you how lost I feel here, how much I hate it here. And still, you never mentioned it!" Tears have sprung into my eyes. I want to wipe them away, but I don't. "Enroll me!"

She has nothing to say to this and frankly, I cannot believe I said it all. It came out almost exactly like I planned it last night (when I couldn't sleep a wink and stayed up rehearsing it).

"I'll wait while you do." I know I'm rude. I can't help it.

"Now, Hannah...." I just sit down, fold my arms. I am a

force to be reckoned with. By the end of first period, Mrs. Schultz has called my mother for permission to enroll me and gotten me into the Project to begin in September. I guess I can deal with a few more months here. Maybe I can deal with anything.

Chapter 34

I cannot believe this! I am seventeen years old and I have to stay with my grandparents. My parents are going away for the weekend and because of what happened, because of the "Blue Bathrobe Incident," they are insisting, in other words, forcing us to go to Grandma and Grandpa's in Long Beach. Poppy and Helen live there, too, but Helen finds it too difficult to have house guests. My parents know how much I hate to stay alone, and due to my lack of friends, I have no one else to stay with. This will be torture.

Grandma and Grandpa live in a one-bedroom apartment overlooking the boardwalk and the ocean. It's the same apartment my father and uncle grew up in. I'd say it must have been a bit crowded back then. My grandmother lies about her age but we think she's actually older than Grandpa, which is pretty old. She wraps everything in wax paper and rubber bands and I mean everything. Forks, knives, spatulas, scissors, you name it, all wrapped up like bizarre Hanukkah presents.

She never kisses us, but sticks her chin out for us to kiss her. Her chin is so long and pointy that we can never get to her cheek and always wind up kissing that sharp protuberance. Last year I had three wisdom teeth removed because the dentist said they might cause my chin to jut out. The thought that I might one day look like my grandmother convinced me to have the surgery, immediately.

They never go to the beach. Even on the hottest day of the summer, but they watch us go from their terrace that looks out from the fifth floor. They wave to us and smile, but will never come down. The beach is way too messy! Before we return to the apartment my grandmother lines the floors leading to the bathroom with newspaper. God forbid there should be one grain of sand entering their apartment. They only live thirty feet from the beach!

They treat themselves to Louis Sherry ice cream once a week and take about 65 pills a day, each. Mostly vitamins. They have bottles everywhere, all nicely wrapped in wax paper and rubber bands. I hope this is the day for the ice cream. My mother never buys Louis Sherry, but we like it.

I must admit, though, my grandmother makes the best pot roast I ever tasted.

My grandfather is a retired pharmacist, but his real passion in life was to be an opera singer. He was good, but not good enough. He keeps a picture of himself as the policeman from the Pirates of Penzance, framed, in the living room. I don't know why. I think it just depresses him. My mother actually saw the play when she was in high school. Before she even met my father. She said Grandpa was the best.

My grandfather likes to belt out notes. He does it constantly and it gets really annoying. He never sings an aria or even a children's song. Just one, long note, then a few minutes later, another, and so on. It's weird. He's kind of an angry man, never having fulfilled his dreams. He sits in his naugahyde chair and when he isn't belting out notes to anyone who'll listen, he plays twentieth-century classical music, which I'm not partial to. He loves Rachmaninoff. And he is forever criticizing my father and his Mozart mania to me. I have to defend my dad, and to be honest, besides James Taylor, John Denver, Joni Mitchell, and Dan Fogelberg, I love Mozart, too. I'd never tell my father, but it's true. Mozart is fun and beautiful, unlike the composers my grandfather is obsessed over. To me, their music is angry, I guess like he is.

It's winter and we can't go to the beach, so there is absolutely nothing to do. I mean that literally. I suppose we could read a book or listen to Shostakovich, but we are beyond bored. The conversation is as boring as the rest of the day. It goes something like this:

Grandpa: How's school?

Us: It's okay.

Grandpa: What are you studying?

Me: Oh, the usual high school stuff. (I don't say crap even though I want to.)

Joni: We're incubating eggs in our class.

Grandma: The price of tuna fish went up to $0.39 at Waldbaums!

Me: Wow.

Grandma: And you should see the price of toilet paper!

Grandpa: What about you, Ruthie?

Ruthie: Nothing much.

Grandma: Your father was quite a student. Better than his brother.

Ruthie: Yeah, we know.

Grandpa: He was valedictorian.

Joni: What's that?

Grandma: Oh and could he play the piano!

Ruthie: I'm taking piano lessons, you know.

Grandma: I need to use the coupons by Sunday or they'll expire.

Me: What do you need to buy, Grandma? (Like I really want to know!)

Grandma: Tuna fish is on sale. There's a sale on Charmin.

How much tuna fish can they eat? And really, how much toilet paper do two people really need? I'll explain valedictorian to Joni later.

Then there's silence while we sit on the couch and wait for what comes next. Oh, here comes some more.

"So you're seventeen, Hannah.

"Yes, I am, Grandpa." Will I get my $15 birthday check? I'm surprised I haven't already received it.

"Now that you're seventeen, what are your plans? Do you still want to be a vet?" Grandpa sounds like he's actually interested.

"Well, I've been thinking about studying environmental science or zoology. I might want to do research in the field, you know, in Africa, or maybe I'll study whales." This is more of a conversation than I can ever remember having with him.

It's kind of neat.

"I doubt you'll do anything of the kind. You'll probably end up a housewife," he says, looking at me.

My jaw drops open as if it is unhinged and I'm staring at him. I think my fists are clenched. I cannot believe he just said that. Even my sisters look shocked. Ruthie looks scared at what might come out of my mouth, and before I have time to count to ten like my mother tells me I'd better, I say, "Who the hell do you think you are to say that!"

Now my grandfather has his mouth open. I see the veins in his forehead begin to radiate. I've never spoken to him this way before but I glare at him and refuse to look away. I will not back down. He sees I'm mean and serious and he swallows hard before looking away.

At this point I've had enough of this and grabbing my coat, I open the door and tell them that I'm going for a walk and out I go. I don't even wait for a response.

Down the mentholated-smelling hallway to the elevator. I feel a little guilty leaving my two sisters in there to languish in the boredom, but not guilty enough to take them with me. There's an old woman with a walker coming as I get in. I don't want to wait for her, but of course I do. She is taking forever to get in! I'm never getting old. No way. Wait, if I don't, that means I'll die young. Okay, I take it back. But I won't get frail and decrepit.

She smiles sweetly at me, and I force a smile back and down we go. When we get to the lobby, I hold the elevator door open for her so she can get out without the thing closing on her.

"Thank you, dear," she says, smiling. I wonder what she

looked like when she was my age. Did she want to be something? And did she become that something? Did her dreams come true?

The last time I was at my grandparents' I found a tiny green bird with a long pointy beak in the lobby. It had probably flown in when the doors were open and in trying to get out through the glass window, nearly killed itself. My parents found a box and let me take it home. I nursed it for two days, feeding it with an eye dropper and caring for it, but it died anyway. I look around the lobby just in case, but there's nothing that needs taking care of.

I leave by the side entrance and walk the twenty steps to the boardwalk ramp and I breathe deeply of the cold salt air. It smells great here. I always forget how much I like coming here. If I can be out in this, that is. My father used to be a Good Humor man riding his ice cream freezer tricycle and ringing his bell. He had a whole section of just the boardwalk. My mother used to meet him here and he'd give her free ice cream. I think that's kind of romantic.

I don't go far. There aren't many people out in this weather, except for the die hard exercise maniacs and a few weirdos sitting on benches, talking to themselves. I just walk a bit and then stand and look out to the sea. It's cold and my hair is blowing, sticky now. I love the ocean. I wish my parents hadn't moved to Westchester, but had stayed here. At least then I could always have the ocean. The ocean seems so vast, that I feel part of something mysterious and great. I wonder what animals are right nearby, under the dark surface. The waves are crashing hard. They always seem to be stronger in the winter. I kind of want to take my shoes off and run on the beach, but first of all, Grandma would have a conniption fit if I did, (no newspaper ready and waiting) and with my luck, I'll find tons of litter, broken glass and cigarette butts. God, I hate finding cigarette butts on the beach, like the beach is a smoker's personal oversized ashtray! I have on occasion mentioned something like that to one or two beach smokers. It's my nature. I can't help it. Really I can't.

The sun is starting to set and it's very pretty, and I'm not that mad anymore. They're probably getting worried, although if they wanted to find me, all they'd have to do is look out the terrace. Here I am! I whistle loudly with my fingers. I learned how to do it two years ago. I taught myself. I practiced for hours, two fingers of each hand touching the top underside of my tongue, and man, can I produce an earsplitting whistle! The very first time I did it, I was holding one of our cats, Calico, and the noise sent her into space.

They don't hear me through the Rachmaninoff. I take a last look at the ocean as the sun moves out of sight and make my way back down the ramp and into the building. I have to ring the buzzer. Ruthie makes sure it's me and I go up. Dinner is probably ready. I hope it's pot roast and I hope there's Louis Sherry ice cream for dessert.

Chapter 35

"Quick, change the channel! Dad's pulling in!" Ruthie screams to me as we lie on our parents' bed watching a re-run of I Love Lucy. The conveyor belt is starting to move faster and Lucy's beginning to stuff chocolate balls into her mouth. This is the best part, of course!

He's early tonight. We usually have time to finish Lucy, but there are episodes we've only heard about and never seen because of him. As it is, he's ruined Dark Shadows for us. When I was younger, our mother had to fight for Bewitched and I Dream of Jeannie, which were our favorites. Nowadays, forget even thinking about Happy Days or Laverne and Shirley!

I quickly change the channel to the local news station as Dad is coming up the stairs and I sit back down on the bed, casually. He smiles as he enters the room and gives each of us a kiss.

"Hello there, girls. Watching the news, I see. Anything interesting happening in the world, Joni?"

"Oh, yes, lots, Dad," Joni says, with all seriousness.

He laughs and takes off his tie and jacket. He is in a good mood tonight. He picks Joni up and twirls her around, then goes into the bathroom.

"Change it back, Hannah, I want to see what Lucy does! I always miss the funny parts." Ruthie, who wants to be a comedian herself, hates to move once she's in TV mode.

But I'm not listening. I am completely focused on what is happening on the screen. My heart starts to race as I am watching this news story. My stomach begins to twist as hundreds of Chinese-looking people climb out of boats. They look emaciated and terrified. They're crying, clinging to each other for dear life.

"I don't want to watch this!" my sisters scream.

"Shut up! I do." I stand up and block the television knobs. I can't look away and I care nothing for Lucy Ricardo at this moment.

The newscaster is standing by one of the boats, his microphone in hand. I focus on what he is saying. "...called 'Boat people,' hundreds of thousands of them are arriving from war-torn Vietnam to the shores of Thailand, Indonesia, Malaysia, Hong Kong, all hoping for a chance to come to America to start a new life. These refugees have suffered hardships unlike anything imaginable. Starvation, unrelenting thirst, piracy, storms. These ramshackle boats were never meant to hold even fifty persons, let alone two hundred plus..."

"Hannah, come on down and set the table." My father is standing in the doorway, towel around his neck, but I ignore him. I'm frozen, standing there with my fists clenched in front of my mouth. He watches with me and soon my mother joins us and we all stand in their bedroom together, watching this tragedy unfold.

I can't move. My face is burning hot with tears and emotion. I can't breathe. I feel all twisted up inside. I don't want anyone to see me.

"What's wrong with you?" Joni asks loudly.

I shoot a glare at her. "Leave me alone," I say. It feels like I'm yelling, but it comes out in a whisper through clenched teeth.

I've seen sad reports on the news before, but this one seems to have punched me right in the stomach. "I've got to do something!" I say, mostly to myself when the news report is over.

I know about Vietnam, the war at least. I was just a little kid when we were fighting over there. I know we didn't win. I wore a silver POW bracelet for years. Major Charles White, Jr. The day he was captured just happened to be my birthday. Weird, huh? I got it when I was ten years old and wore it until I was almost fourteen. I found out that he eventually made it home. I even wrote to him. My mother told me not to expect an answer. That he was probably traumatized. I never did get a response. I still have the bracelet in my top drawer. I look at it once in a while, wondering about him.

Someone turns off the TV and my parents and sisters leave the room to go down for dinner, but I just stand there, statue-like, staring at the television screen. All I can see are those desperate faces and the thought of them suffering like that makes my insides flip. My pounding heart slows a little but I still I feel like throwing up. I sit on the edge of the bed and catch a breath. It feels calming. I take another one.

"I've got to do something," I whisper to myself again. I am determined and suddenly there's a different feeling happening inside me that I can't explain. Whatever it is, it feels almost good.

"Mom, Dad, who do you think I should call?" I ask when I finally can move and go downstairs.

"Call about what?" my father says, his mouth full of London broil he's grabbed from the sizzling pan.

"About the Boat People! I've got to do something!"

"Hannah, what do you think you can do? Stop being so impulsive."

My mother looks at him pleadingly. "If Hannah wants to help, we can give her some suggestions." I know the look. Don't sabotage Hannah's idea. We've got to do something to make her happy.

"Right, right," he agrees, but I know he thinks I'm crazy. I see him shake his head as he walks to the table.

"Do you think calling CBS would be a good idea?" I ask, but I already know it is.

"Well, I guess you could do that. That was the station that aired the report, wasn't it? Sure, I think it's a fine idea. Though I doubt anyone will be there now. Try on Monday."

I'm sure he's right and for the first time, I wish it wasn't Friday. Monday can't come fast enough.

I go to bed thinking about working with the Boat People. I imagine myself helping people out of boats on some distant shore, reaching my hand in to help those weary travelers. I drift off to sleep, the harsh images of the painful faces I've seen on the news mixing with visions of smiling refugee children looking gratefully up at me.

Part 3 - Encounters

Mei

Chapter 36

Everything moves so fast here, I am afraid I will never adjust. Marion, our caseworker from the International Rescue Committee who met us at the airport was so kind and welcoming to us, I wish we could have stayed with her. She brought with her some old coats, which we accepted gratefully. We put them on before we stepped out into the New York afternoon, which was colder than anything we had ever experienced in our lives. In the van, waiting for us, was Danh, a Vietnamese refugee himself who has been here for three years and now works as a translator for IRC.

We three looked out the van window as we drove over a bridge that looked onto the city skyline, marveling at the size of it, the tallness of the buildings seeming to touch the sky. How I want to paint that skyline and send it to my parents!

There were many cars following us into the area we will

now call home. Our new neighborhood is a somewhat dirty place, in an area of New York called Bronx. Our street is off the main thoroughfare and is tightly crowded with many apartment buildings, all about six storeys high. Our building is crumbling a bit, but it will be home. I am not complaining, but it is unlike what I had imagined. But then I think again, are dreams really anything like what the reality brings?

Before taking us to our apartment, Marion and Danh bring us first to a small market near our building where they purchase rice, eggs, some meat and vegetables, cooking oil, coffee, tea, toilet paper, soap and juice to drink. Then they take us to the second floor apartment, our home, and give me the key as well as a bag filled with cooking utensils and chopsticks. They stay for about thirty minutes, telling us how to get to the IRC office in Manhattan, how to use the stove and bathroom shower. Our apartment has four rooms, one of which is a small kitchen with a large refrigerator, a gas stove which has been only lightly cleaned and an old table with two well used chairs.

There is a living room with a very old sofa next to a large window with no curtain on it, overlooking the street. There are two tiny bedrooms, each with what looks like a new mattress on the floor with sheets and comforters folded neatly on them. There are three pillows as well. I wonder what kind IRC worker brought those here and I say a silent grateful prayer. There is a bathroom with a tub and shower which I long to climb into and soak in scalding hot water! We do not have to share this place with anyone else. The IRC has paid our first month's rent and will help us until we get settled. Marion knows we have many family members more to come, so it is ours alone, hopefully soon to be filled with the rest of our family. I ask her when I can file for sponsorship for my family, and through Danh's translation, she tells me we first must relax, allow ourselves to adjust, and that we will have jet-lag, something people get after being on airplanes for long periods of time, crossing datelines and time zones. We should come to her office in Manhattan in a few days. Linh is asleep on the mattress even before they leave. Again, Danh gives us directions to their office and they say goodbye, that there are other arrivals coming later.

And now, here, alone in our new apartment, I am fearful of every sound, every bellow from above or below. There are other refugees in this building, four other families I was told. I do not know if we have anything in common, but it is reassuring to know they are here. Thankfully it is very warm inside, for outside we were chilled to the bone.

Our first night is terrifying, although nothing untoward happens at all. The door has a chain and a lock and I put one of the kitchen chairs in front of it. There are sounds of sirens all night, some close and some off in the distance. I wonder how many criminals are abroad on the streets this cold night. I huddle under the blanket with Linh by my side, and my brother, who should have been sleeping on his own mattress, comes rushing in, climbing in with us. We stay awake for a long time, listening to the sounds of the New York night, starting at every loud sound. Banging noises come from the large metal radiators, but we soon realize it is only their way of sending heat from them, and for that we are very grateful. As we settle into restless sleep, we whisper thanks to Kuan Yin for keeping us together and keeping us safe and for having someone waiting for us when we arrived.

Our first few days, it seems Marion is right. We sleep at strange daylight hours and awaken in the darkness, feeling disoriented and heavy-lidded. We are almost normal now and ready to visit Marion and Danh in their office in Manhattan, a long bus ride from here. I want to ask for a telephone so that I can call my parents. I want to enroll my brother in school. I want to buy fabric to make curtains for privacy. Today, we will go downstairs to visit our refugee neighbors, and hopefully they will help us. I wonder if they were as fearful as I am when they first arrived.

I knock on their door and a little girl of about two stands in front of her mother, a young woman, a little older than I. She smiles broadly, her teeth blackened, and extends her hand in greeting. We enter and find many people, some family members, some from the other families from other apartments, sitting on the floor together. We spend the afternoon telling each other stories of our experiences, speaking in a mix of Vietnamese and Chinese. The young woman and her husband have only arrived several weeks ago, but they know how to get to Marion's office and will accompany us tomorrow.

I look around to see if there is a telephone and to my dismay, there is not. I will ask tomorrow. I am served sunflower seeds and cà phê phin and as I sit drinking it with them in their warm living room, sitting on the floor, I realize that one of my dreams has come true. Linh is playing with the toddlers and my brother is listening intently to the men's tales of the camps.

The young woman takes me aside and tells me that she

does not like it here, that she is afraid all the time. Her husband goes to work and leaves her alone with their baby, and she only wants to lock the door and stay inside. Her caseworker is a good woman, she says, but it is far to get to her office and she hasn't much time to spend, as there are so many refugees coming and she is very busy with them.

She takes my arm and says she is glad for a friend. I cannot reassure her, as I am also very much afraid but I smile and say, yes, I, too, am glad to have a friend.

Hannah

Chapter 37

"You know, Hannah, this is a wonderful piece of writing. Why is this the first time I've seen something like this from you?" Miss Tyler, my English teacher, is a tiny, gray-haired older woman who wears pleated skirts and high-neck blouses and constantly reads us poetry. Most of the students sit at their desks, chewing gum or writing notes to each other, not paying a bit of attention, but I like the way she is so into what she's reading. For such a plain and almost timid-looking woman, she is fiery about writing.

She is supposedly married to Ms. Bruno, the typing teacher. Ms. Bruno looks like her name sounds. Big and dark and mannish. No one can figure out how she can type on those small typewriters with her beefy fingers, but she does all right. 110 words per minute, or so she likes to brag. Everyone makes fun of the two of them, but I think Miss Tyler is a pretty good teacher, and not just because she likes my writing. She's introduced me to Edna Saint Vincent Millay, and for that I'm very grateful. "Ballad of the Harp Weaver." Wow.

"I don't know. I guess I didn't have anything to say before."

"I think you should publish this in Golden Wings."

Golden Wings is our school newspaper. When I was in seventh grade, before my friends all hit the road, I thought about being on the high school newspaper staff. We'd all be in the newsroom, discussing hot topics, the intellectual elite. I thought I'd take stunning photos and write pithy articles about the goings on at school and around the world.

But that was before. Now I have no desire to share my thoughts, feelings, poems or prose with anyone from this school. Maybe when I get to the Project I'll show them what I can do. Maybe they'll want to see the pictures I take or read what I write. The only reason Miss Tyler got to see my real writing self is because it was a good assignment and I actually had something to say. And anyway, I wrote it for myself, not for anybody else.

"Would you read it aloud to the class?" She knows I barely say a word in her class, even though I am often bursting with things I want to say; smart things, funny things. I don't mind sharing this with her, but I'm not going to humiliate myself by revealing any part of me with any stinking person in this trap.

"No thanks, Miss Tyler. It's not all that good, anyway."

"Well, you're wrong about that, Hannah. Hence the A+. I don't give out grades like that as a matter of course."

"Yeah, I know. Thanks. But sorry, I just can't."

"Would you let me?"

"No, I don't know, maybe. Only if it's anonymous. How's that?"

"I suppose I could keep the identity of the author to myself, if that is truly your wish."

At this point, I *truly* don't care. It's just an essay about what I saw on the news the other night. I'm probably the only person in my class who spends even a minute thinking about people from Vietnam. They'll just think I'm weird, as usual. Right now I'm really hungry, which is a first, and I have a sandwich in my locker that I really would like to try and eat. I feel like I'm just killing time in school today, just waiting until 3:00 so I can leave this place, drive home and call the TV station. I missed my chance yesterday. I had therapy. That was fun.

"So, Hannah, how are you feeling today? Any thoughts you want to share?"

I tell Mrs. Rosenkrantz about my idea and that I'm pissed off that I have to be here instead of calling CBS like I really want to.

"The refugees aren't going anywhere, Hannah. There will be time tomorrow to call. I think it is wonderful that you are passionate about this issue."

"Yeah, but I'm sure everyone else will think I'm totally odd."

"Do you really care what they think?" She gives me this look that tells me she knows my answer.

"I guess not."

"I know not. Hannah, you are a most independent spirit. You follow your convictions even if it means you won't be popular. One

day, there will be those who appreciate this quality."

"Yeah, maybe. But right now, no one appreciates anything about me. It's beyond not being popular, Mrs. Rosenkrantz. It's about being an outcast."

My English teacher is waiting for my answer. She is standing there, delicate arms folded across her chest, wanting me to give her permission to let others in on my private thoughts. Why not, who cares?

"Okay, Miss Tyler, if you really want to. Sure, go ahead. Just please, do not mention my name."

She smiles at me, raising her gray eyebrows. I know what she's thinking; Hannah knows it's a good piece of writing and if she had any friends at all, she'd be glad to share it with them. If she had any confidence at all, she'd be proud of this fine piece of prose.

Maybe she's right. Maybe I am proud of it, but I'd never admit it to anyone. I wrote it only to please myself anyway. I don't care what anybody thinks. I want to show it to my mother.

"I'd like to bring it home, first."

"Of course, why don't I just Xerox it, would that be all right, dear?"

Miss Tyler calls everybody dear. The moronic girls in the class think she's making passes at them when she says this. She's not, believe me. I tell her it would be fine and she goes to the Xerox machine in the main office while I wait in the room. Her grade book is open on her desk. I can't help it. I peer over and see the grades for this assignment. I am the only "A+" let alone "A." I flip the page to Amy's class. Amy:

"C-," Tracy: "C+." Just checking.

There are still two more hours of this school day and I'm itching to get out of here. I want to cut class and head home, but I know I won't. I'm not the cutting-class type. I have been called goody-goody. I'm not. I'm conscientious, I guess. Is that a terrible thing? It's definitely not popular, but as Mrs. Rosenkrantz said, there will one day be someone who appreciates me for it. I'd like to know when.

Mei

Chapter 38

We are dressed in our large overcoats and look ridiculous as we make our way out of our building and to the bus stop. I am freezing cold and terrified as I see all the people getting on this bus and hear them talking loudly and quickly in this language I cannot understand. Linh grips my hand as we climb on. My new friend and her husband are taking us to Marion's office. They show us how to put coins she counted out before we left into the slot. Linh smiles as they clink and rattle their way down.

We find a seat but not together. My brother stands in front of us, guarding us, the young woman and her husband and baby across the aisle and down a few seats. I try not to take my eyes off them, fearing they will get off and leave us, but I am fascinated by all the faces I see before me; some dark brown, others pale as a morning sky, mostly all bundled against the cold, some talking to each other, others silent, thinking their private thoughts. As I watch them, I become less afraid. We are all people, different perhaps, but all with thoughts and feelings and ideas, plans.

We arrive in Manhattan and walk several blocks to Marion's office. She greets us with the same warmth she extended when she first met us. Danh comes in to translate and I am overwhelmed with all the information I must take in. Where to enroll my brother at school, where to study English if I choose to, where to get stamps that will help to pay for our food, where to find a job. My mind is reeling as I take in this information and wish my father was here to take over. I do not want all this responsibility, but I shake myself clear and stop my mind from swirling. I focus on what Marion and Danh are saying; I take a piece of paper and pen and write down instructions. I can tell Marion sees my distress and she takes a deep breath and comes over, placing her hand on my shoulder. She tells me everything will be all right. I smile at her and try to believe that.

We fill out papers that will be filed with the UNHCR so that my family will be reunited, and I want to burn some incense and send my prayers across the sea to them so that we will find each other. And soon.

Marion will help me get a telephone installed in my apartment and try to find a kind volunteer who might be able to help us get adjusted to our new life here. That would be a lucky thing. I will pray for it.

Mostly, though, I guiltily wish she could get me a set of paints and brushes so that I could lose myself and these responsibilities for just a moment. So that I can again feel the strength of the wooden brush as it slips into the clear water and then again into the paints, creating beauty out of nothing but horsehair and color.

Hannah

Chapter 39

I am shaking as I call directory assistance.

"Directory assistance. What city please?" the operator asks.

"New York City. CBS television, please," I say, my heart beating rapidly.

"The number is…"

I write down the number and then call the station. I ask the receptionist to connect me with someone about that news story. No one is available so I ask her if she has any information about where someone would call if they wanted to volunteer. She suggests I call the United Nations. Why didn't I think of that?

I call 411 again and get the number. Dad will probably kill me. I think it costs a dollar every time you call it. I scribble it down and then I sit down. Hard. What am I doing? What if they don't take me seriously? I'm seventeen, for God's sake! What can I do? This is stupid. Retarded! Now I feel embarrassed. What the hell was I thinking? Like anybody from the U.N. is going to give a job to a seventeen-year-old eleventh grader. Right. Moron.

I put the phone back on its bright yellow cradle and leave the kitchen. I walk around the house, pacing back and forth. I just feel dumb. Thank God I didn't embarrass myself. At least the operator won't think twice. She probably thinks my father works there and I needed the number. Who am I kidding? She probably didn't think about it for a nanosecond after I hung up. Does anybody really care what I do? And why do I care so much what everybody else thinks? Now I'm getting angry. At myself mostly. Mrs. Rosenkrantz thought my idea was great. What's wrong with a seventeen-year-old young woman wanting to help some refugees? Nothing, that's what, God damn it!

I pick up the phone again, but this time I'm not breathing hard or having an anxiety attack. I dial the number.

"United Nations, where may I direct your call?" The woman who answers the phone has a very dignified accent, maybe French.

"Um, I'd like to speak to someone in charge of refugee affairs." I try to sound if not official, at least intelligent.

"Hold, please." Silence for twenty seconds, then a man gets on the line.

"How can I help you?" American accent this time.

"Uh, are you in charge of refugee affairs?"

"No. Sorry. With whom do you wish to speak?"

"I want to speak to someone about refugees."

"Hold, please." More silence. I almost hang up, but then another man picks up, this time definitely foreign.

"Hello."

"Hello," I say, wondering who he's going to connect me with.

"What can I do for you?"

"I was wondering if you might need any volunteers to work with the Boat People, you know, Vietnamese refugees." There, I said it.

"You know, I wish I could help you, but right now we're not dealing with refugees. Sorry."

"Oh." I must sound crestfallen because he says brightly, "Hang on a minute, I have an idea."

I hear him speaking to someone, but it's muffled. Five seconds later he's back. "Miss?"

"Yes, I'm still here." Now my heart is starting to beat quickly again.

"I'm going to give you the name of an organization that might be able to help you. Do you have a pencil?"

"Yes."

"It's the International Rescue Committee. IRC." He gives me the phone number and the address in New York City. I thank him and before he hangs up, he says, "How old are you, if you don't mind me asking?"

"Seventeen," I tell him.

"Wonderful. What you want to do, I mean. Thank you." He's thanking me. I smile to myself. Wow.

I look at the number on my scrap of paper. I pick up the phone again. Dial.

"International Rescue Committee. Where can I direct your

call?"

"Refugee affairs," I say for the fourth time today.

"From what country?"

They must work with refugees from all over the world.

"Vietnam," I tell her.

"Hold, please."

A woman with a thick accent answers the phone. I think she is Vietnamese. Here goes. I ask to speak to someone in charge of volunteers, if there is such a person.

"Marion is in charge. You hold while I get her." I'm about to speak to Marion! A real refugee worker! I don't have to wait long.

"Hello, this is Marion. Can I help you?"

"Hi, my name is Hannah and I saw a report on the news the other night about the Boat People and I'd like to help, if I could." Did I say that right? Did I sound stupid?

"Hi, Hannah. That's wonderful. Volunteers are very few and far between, so anyone willing to help is really appreciated. I'll tell you what we need." Oh, I know I'm going to get an assignment, maybe to go to one of the camps.

"We need donations; you know, like, clothing, dishes, furniture, that sort of thing. You could call some local churches or synagogues and ask them. They're usually pretty generous."

"Uh, all right. I guess I could do that." I'm sure she hears the disappointment in my voice.

I hear her smiling as she asks, "Hannah, do you have a car?" Oh, thank you Poppy! Yes, I do! I do!

"Yes, I do."

"Well, there is one thing you might be able to help us with.

We've got five families in the Bronx who could use a friend."

My heart is in my throat. I can barely speak. I am overwhelmed.

"Hello? Hannah?"

"Yes, I'm here," I say, practically choking. "I would love to work with five families in the Bronx." I really would. I cannot believe this.

Marion gives me directions to her office on Park Avenue. We make an appointment for a few weeks from now. She's really busy so she can't meet any sooner. I can't wait! I'll be there. Maybe I'll cut school that day. Maybe not.

In the meantime, Marion tells me to start asking for donations. She says that's very important, too. Lots of families are arriving.

I call the temple where I was confirmed last year. They're nice and say they'd love to help. They tell me to come to the synagogue for Friday night services and I can make my announcement then.

"What announcement?" I ask.

"Of course you have to tell the congregation what you're doing. It'll sound better coming directly from the horse's mouth," the Rabbi's secretary tells me.

Oh, just great. Public speaking is not one of my strong suits. But for this, I'll do it.

Friday comes soon enough and I put on a skirt and blouse and tell my parents where I'm going. My dad asks me if it's all right if he comes along. I really don't want him there, I don't really want to speak in front of anyone I know, but he looks so happy that I'm going to temple and says he'd like to go to services, so I agree. He's still in his suit, so we leave right away. He lets me drive.

We enter the synagogue and I look around at all the faces. There are mostly old people, or people my dad's age. Some of the men take the black, silky yarmulkes out of the basket, but some are wearing beautifully colored ones they probably got when they went to Israel. My father hasn't been to Israel so he pulls one from the basket. I take one too and put it on my head. I've seen girls do that before, and I don't know why, but tonight, it just feels right. I see a girl I know from my confirmation class sitting with her parents. She gives me a pleading look and I smile at her.

My father and I sit on the aisle in the middle of the hall. He's holding my hand as we sit there, waiting for the service to begin. The Rabbi makes some general announcements and asks if there is anything anyone would like to share. One person gets up and tells about an upcoming fund raiser, another about a youth group field trip. I wait until everyone is done and then stand up. I'm shaking and my heart is in my mouth.

"Um, I'd like to make an announcement. I'll be working with refugees from Vietnam and they need all kinds of things, like clothing, dishes, appliances, stuff like that. So if you have anything you'd like to donate, that'd be great. Please bring whatever you want to give to the Rabbi's office. Thank you."

I sit down harder than I planned to. My palms are sweaty and I can feel that my face is probably beet red. My father pats my hand and we sit through the service, but I'm not listening. I'm going over and over in my head the words I said, wondering if I sounded stupid.

My confirmation teacher comes up to me after the service is over and asks me exactly what I'll be doing. I tell her and she smiles and says, "Oh, Hannah, you could have done this four years ago when you were thirteen; it could have served as your mitzvah project." That's the act of charity every Bat or Bar Mitzvah is supposed to do before they get Bat Mitzvahed. But I'd decided I didn't want to have a Bat Mitzvah. I know it was a disappointment to everyone, especially my grandparents. I felt bad, but not bad enough to go through with it. I had my reasons. First of all, I basically failed Hebrew school. I just couldn't get it. We weren't learning what the words meant, just how to read them. I mean, what was the point? If I was going to pray, I wanted to know what I was praying about. I'm not even sure the Hebrew teacher understood what she was reading.

Plus, I got really turned off when my Sunday school class had to watch the film Night and Fog. It was the most disturbing film I have ever seen. I could not understand why a bunch of twelve and thirteen-year old Jewish kids had to watch a documentary film showing actual footage from the Holocaust. I mean actual. I'm talking emaciated bodies and lampshades with numbers on them and human hair stuffing for pillows and mass graves and more emaciated bodies. Never forget. Well, I never did. I couldn't sleep for about a year after watching that film. I didn't even want to get out of bed. I kept imagining all those bodies were on the floor of my bedroom. Maybe racists should see it or the grandchildren of Nazis. Or maybe everybody should see it when they grow up! But why us? Why then? I mean, those images are still there, in my head.

Anyway, my parents were so disappointed that I refused to have a Bat Mitzvah that they begged me to get confirmed when I was sixteen. I did and to tell you the truth, I really am proud of my Jewish heritage. It feels good being part of a tradition that goes back more than five thousand years. I like the culture. I like being connected to people who have always been survivors.

A few people come up to me and my dad after the service and tell me they've got an old toaster, some clothes their kid outgrew, an old bed. One woman even shakes my hand and says I'm a mensch, whatever that is. My father sees my confusion and tells me it's a Yiddish word for a good-deed-doer. My dad and I walk out of the temple and he puts his arm around me and tells me he's proud of me. Lots of Jews are philanthropists, he tells me. I guess you're one too, he says. I guess.

We live three doors down from a Protestant church so I go there, too. They know me well because I was a member of the Bell Choir when I was nine. My parents let me join. It was fun. All the neighborhood kids were in the Bell Choir. It didn't matter what religion you were. You just rang the bells. There was Luisa, who was a Colombian Catholic girl whose father was the church caretaker. Terry, an Episcopalian; Nan, whose father was an atheist, and me, a Jew. There were others, but I can't remember them all.

We all rang those bells like crazy and then when we were finished we'd all play in the churchyard behind the church. It has this enormous Copper Beech tree, the biggest tree you've ever seen, with a tire swing hanging from it. People carve their initials into it, but I never did and no matter how many boyfriends I ever have, if any, I never will. I think it's cruel.

I go to the office of the church and tell them what I'm

doing. They also are happy to give what they can. They have a little tag sale they do once a month and they invite me to come and take what I like. I think that's neat!

My mom and I go through our house, and start to fill a big black garbage bag full of old clothes that we've outgrown. My mom has lots of mismatched plates she's willing to give and some shoes she doesn't like anymore. I head into my sisters' room where Joni is on the floor playing with some dolls. I ask her if she has any toys she'd like to donate. Joni goes over to her toy box and sits down on it.

"Nope," she says, "Nothing."

"I can't believe you're so selfish," I tell her. She gives me a dirty look and I realize that she probably has no idea of what I'm about to do. She is only eight. I decide to change tactics and say in a really nice voice, "Joni, you know I'll be working with kids who have absolutely nothing. They are very poor and could use some toys to play with. It would be a really nice thing to do. Do you really need everything in that toy box? Don't you want to help children who have nothing?"

That seems to work and she nods and slowly opens the wooden top. We look inside and there is a lot of stuff she no longer plays with. She goes through each and every one, weighing each decision carefully. Then she hands over one thing after another.

"Tell them they're from me."

"Sure, but maybe you'll be able to tell them yourself." She smiles at me.

One bag, half full. Loads more to go! And I can't wait.

Meí

Chapter 40

Today is the first day my brother will not be with us. He will be at school. He wakes himself this morning before the sun, bathes and slicks his hair back, putting on his finest clothes. Of course he has no fine clothes, but at least his clothes are clean and pressed. I wake up early to make breakfast for him, but he is too excited to eat the rice gruel I prepare. I have bought him a small book bag and in it I have placed a notebook and a pen. The bag is already slung over his shoulder and it is not yet seven a.m.

Linh stumbles into the kitchen, her black hair tousled and in her face. She is smiling. She knows we will be taking a walk to Tuan's school this morning. Linh so wants to go to school, but she is too young yet to attend, but at least she will get to see what an American school looks like.

"I want a school bag, like Tuan!" she demands, seeing the

one he carries.

We have no money for unnecessary items and though I wish I could have gotten one for her, I could not. Tuan, good boy that he is, takes his bag and places it over her shoulder and says, "You may carry this to school for me today."

"And when we pick you up later?"

"Of course," he replies.

Linh smiles broadly and begins to promenade proudly around the apartment, her little chest out, her shoulders back.

Coats on, we head out the door at 7:30, into the cold morning, another new adventure for us. We walk the many blocks to the school without much trouble, as we have practiced this walk several times; once when we enrolled him, and twice more just to make sure. When we arrive, we stand at the entrance, unable to move. There are many, many children, mostly Tuan's age, congregating by a high fence. Some are chatting with each other, some are playing basketball, others are looking suspicious, cigarettes dangling from their mouths. A few look us over, then return to their conversations. I want to grab my brother and run back to our apartment, but he takes his book bag from Linh, quickly nods at us and boldly walks into the courtyard where he waits with the others.

I watch him go, envying his courage, hoping he will find a friend amidst all the students here. I search the crowd for an Asian face and see one or two, but not many, and then the bell rings and everyone files inside. Tuan does not look back at us, but moves confidently forward. We watch him enter the building.

Linh waves at the crowd, although Tuan cannot see her. No one waves back and I take her hand and pull her along.

Hannah

Chapter 41

This week takes forever and I'm starting to get sick. I cannot get sick, I tell myself. All I can think about is my meeting with Marion. Will she have photos of the families or just names? Will they be there at her office? Will they know about me when I arrive? I keep picturing what it's going to be like when I meet these refugees. That first knock at the door, the first introductions. How happy they'll be when I give them all the stuff I'm collecting.

So far I've collected ten big black garbage bags full of clothes, winter coats, pots and pans, dish towels and bath towels, sheets and some old blankets, a partial set of silverware. Some old lady from the temple donated her hot curlers and some eye makeup still in its original case, unused. The teachers at the nursery school at the church donated paper and crayons. I got a toaster that works, a set of blue-flowered dishes, two lamps, and a set of yellowing curtains, rods and all. Poppy donated a stack of toothbrushes, some toothpaste and a box of plastic rings for the kids. Dad gave me a stack of yellow legal pads and a couple of boxes of pens from his office, and an old electric typewriter.

Miss Tyler read my story today. I left the room, telling her I had go to the nurse, but she knew why I was getting out of there. I couldn't believe she was going to read it right in front of me.

I came back when I thought she'd be finished, but she wasn't. And I couldn't just walk out again. Thankfully she didn't give me a look as I sat down. And as she finished it, I looked around through my veil of long hair, and I saw that every face was looking at her and they were actually paying attention. A few kids clapped. I was astonished. Maybe I underestimate some of the people here.

I drive home, feeling absolutely horrible. I am sure I have a fever and when I get home, my mother takes my temperature, and I do: a hundred and three. I get into bed and that's when the coughing starts. I can barely sleep all night, and there is no way I'm going to school the next day. I've got to get well. I cannot miss my meeting with Marion!

In the morning, my father tries to get me to go to school, telling me that he goes to work even with a temperature, that I should will myself to be well and stop coughing. I force out a really heinous cough, one that sounds like I have tuberculosis, causing my father to roll his eyes toward the ceiling and leave the room. He does this every time one of us gets sick. He can't stand it when we're sick. It seems to make him angry, as if we're doing it on purpose, as if we're weak-willed and let it happen. Not that I care if I miss a day or even a week at that school. But I really hope I'm well soon. I don't want to be hacking away in Marion's office.

I lie in my parents' bed, like I always do when I'm sick, watching Days of Our Lives. Flora, our once-a-week housekeeper is ironing in front of the TV. She loves to watch soaps while she irons. She got me hooked on this one, but the only time I can watch it is when I'm sick or when there's a day off from school. And no matter how long I haven't seen it, I can always get right back into the story. But today, I really don't feel good and even watching makes my head ache. I still have a fever and the cough hurts. Every once in a while, my mother comes up with a cup of tea and rubs Vicks on my chest.

I can't turn off the TV because Flora can't iron without it, and the only place she irons is right here in my parents' bedroom. I suppose I could move back into my own room, but it feels too lonely in there. Anyway, I like the way the room smells like hot cotton and steam. I like the way Flora gets all the creases and wrinkles out of all those white collared shirts. I like Flora, but I hate the fact that we have a maid. My mother says she's not a maid, but a housekeeper, and that she's in nursing school, so that she can better herself. What's wrong if we can afford to help her, give her a job?

I guess there's nothing wrong with it, but it makes me feel ashamed somehow. I once talked to Flora about it. She looked at me, her head tilted sideways and said, "There's nothing shameful in it. Your parents treat me right. I like what I do. There's nothing undignified in cleaning someone's house and helping out. Why do you think there is?" I couldn't answer, so I dropped the subject, but I don't know. I just find it strange.

Flora's been working for us for nearly five years. Her last name is Johnson and when we first met her, my mom introduced her as Mrs. Johnson, but she insisted we call her by her first name. And that's okay with me. We call all my parents' friends by their first names. I wish I knew her better, but she's pretty private. I know she loves horror films, though. She took me to the movies once, to see her favorite, *The Exorcist*. I never told her that I couldn't sleep for weeks after I saw that film.

She's been around for lots of stuff that goes on in our family; fights and sickness, birthdays once in a while, if they fall on a Thursday, operations. Last year when I had my three wisdom teeth removed, she helped get me to the car. Sounds simple and I don't remember all of it, but she tells me it was the hardest thing she's ever done. The doctor had given my mother some pre-op painkillers to give me, to be taken a few hours before the actual surgery. I took them and I really didn't feel a thing until it was time to get into the car. I remember my mother calling me, telling me to come on. And I remember trying to get out of bed, trying really hard, but nothing worked. My arms and legs were like lead weights and I just could not move. My mother came up and demanded I hurry up; we were going to be late. I just lay there, helpless. I don't think she believed me and she kept trying to force me out of bed. And then I started to laugh. It was the kind of laugh that once you get going, you can't stop. I was hysterical. And the more she tried to force me, the harder I laughed. Finally Flora, who is a really big woman, came to give my mother a hand with me. I was a dead, laughing weight as she hoisted me over her shoulder like a sack of potatoes. I think she was mad that I was laughing like I was, but I couldn't help it. And I kept sliding off her shoulders, onto the floor. When we got as far as the top of the stairs, Flora held me under my armpits, while my mother guided me by the legs, and I bumped and laughed all the way down the stairs. I lay there in a heap, hysterical, finding everything hilarious. The two of them dragged me to the car, my mother holding my legs, Flora my arms, and then shoved me into the front seat and buckled me in. I'm sure my mother would have loved for Flora to come along to the doctor's office, but she didn't ask and by the time we got to the office, I could move a bit on my own. But not by much and I literally crawled from the parking lot to the elevator, where my mother shoved me in with her foot, practically kicking me. I was still laughing when we arrived on the third floor, thankfully directly into the waiting room. My mother pushed and rolled me onto the office floor, cringing, because there were other people waiting.

Flora took care of me when I came back late that afternoon. I guess my parents paid her to stay late, and maybe she wanted to practice her nursing skills. She scolded me gently for the trouble I caused them that morning, but she wasn't too hard on me, seeing how much pain I was in.

She finishes ironing and seeing me falling in and out of sleep, gently turns off the TV set and puts the blankets over me. She pets my hair and leaves the room, shutting the door. By the time I wake up, Flora is gone and my sisters are home from school, making noise. It's the time of day I like the most, that time just before dinner, when it's starting to get dark. When my house smells like cooking and my father comes home from work. I can smell chicken soup, the kind my mother makes when we're sick, with lots of dill and turnips. No one has come to see me and I want them to. I try to call out, but this leads to a coughing fit, but mission accomplished, my mom is there bringing me a bowl of steaming soup, my sisters tagging along behind.

Mei

Chapter 42

I dreamed of my family. We are all at home; the home I remember from before things became dire. I walk through the rooms as if I were really there. I feel the smooth wood of the floors beneath my bare feet, I touch the soft cotton quilt on my small bed. In my dream, I long to climb into that bed.

My mother sits at the kitchen table in front of a steaming bowl of soup, frowning at me, looking disappointed.

"What have I done to displease you, Mother?" I ask her.

She opens her mouth to speak, but words come out in a language I do not understand. Her mouth moves differently with these strange words, and suddenly I realize she is speaking English. I do not know what she is saying and I feel ashamed for not studying harder at the camp. Abruptly, she stops talking and begins to drink her soup, turning away from me. My father walks into the room, shaking his finger, pointing at me.

"Please tell me what I have done to displease you!" I cry, hearing my own voice echoing through the room. At that point my brothers and sisters all gather around the table. Tuan and Linh are among them. Each and every one of them is crying silent tears.

"I've petitioned for all of you to come here! I have! What more do you want me to do?" I am shouting in my dream, but no one seems to be able to answer.

They all sit down at the polished table, bowls of soup appearing before them brimming with noodles and fish. They eat their soup silently, but their eyes look at me over their bowls. And all their eyes look reproachful.

No bowl of soup for me, I notice. And then I awaken in the dark, like I have done so many nights. I cannot return to sleep. Is something wrong? Did I give the correct information to Marion? What if the information arrived too late and they are already in France or Australia and will never come? What if we might never be reunited? I lay frozen in fear upon my mattress until the first light creeps in the window. I get up and go to the bathroom to wash my face. The face reflecting back at me from the mirror is haggard. My hand is balled into a fist knowing it cannot paint my bleak feelings into some expression. I have no paints.

So I quietly pace the floor of the apartment, not wanting to wake my siblings. It is very early. I know what I must do. I find a sheet of paper and a pen, sit down at the table and try to write a letter.

I write: My dear family, we are here in New York, in America. Linh, Tuan and I. We are in a place called Bronx. We live in a building with other Vietnamese families, so I feel very safe. (Of course this is not true, but it is what they need to hear.) I have petitioned for all of you through IRC and UNHCR, so I know we will find each other soon. We must. (Again, I cannot be sure, but these lies make me feel stronger and so I will believe them, truth or no.)

I have a job and Tuan is enrolled in school. Linh stays with our neighbor and her little girl when I am working. She was skinny when we arrived but is getting a little fatter. There are shops here selling food, so we are not hungry. Our caseworker is very kind. I miss you all so very…

This is where I can no longer see the paper. My eyes are filled with tears. I push the paper aside, and lay my head on my folded arms on the table and weep until I have no tears left. I have awakened my little sister who comes shuffling into the room. She puts an arm around my shoulder and climbs onto my lap. She uses her sleeve to wipe my tears and snuggles into me. She says nothing, but her actions are filled with meaning and I take comfort from them. And I am so very grateful to have such a sister as she. I encircle her with my arms, my head against hers and together, we fall in and out of a light sleep this way, in this hard kitchen chair. Perhaps it is a small dream during a moment of sleep, perhaps it is only my imagination, but for an instant I clearly see my mother's face smiling, her eyes filled with approval. My sorrow lifts and I am filled with gratitude. I hug my sister tighter. She hugs me back.

Hannah

Chapter 43

I cut last period today. It's gym, so I'm not real worried about it and anyway I'm still coughing, so I shouldn't be exercising. I drive myself to the train station and buy my round trip ticket for Grand Central Station. I can't believe my appointment is finally here and I'm going to meet Marion!

The express train only takes a little more than half an hour and it's not a far walk to IRC. I bring a notebook and a pen and write down questions I have. I have a lot, like how many people are there in these five families? How long have they been here? Do they know anything at all about life here? Where in the Bronx do they live? Are they near each other? Are they friends or family? What's the most important thing they'll need from me? I'm thinking of lots of questions as we pull into the station. The train lurches to a halt and the doors open. I step out onto the musty platform. I've heard that people live deep in the bowels of Grand Central, that there are entire communities down there. I'm sure I don't want to run into any and since I've never taken the subway by myself before, I walk the twelve or so blocks to Park Avenue and 28th Street.

It's almost three fifteen and my appointment is at three thirty, so I'm walking pretty quickly. Also, it's really cold out. But I don't want to be huffing and coughing when I get there, so I pace myself. I want to make a good impression.

I arrive right on time and enter the building. The whole place is IRC. There's a doorman and I sign in with him and he directs me to the third floor, Vietnamese refugee affairs. I peek at the board before I get on the elevator. There are a lot of different countries listed on that board. I get into the elevator and I'm glad to see one of those elevator men in a uniform, pulling shut the gated door and turning the big brass handle. There are two other people getting in as well. One of them looks Asian. Is he a refugee? I wonder.

Mine is the first stop and I get out, my heartbeat speeding up. I mean, it's kind of like a job interview. I'm sure they're not going to let just anyone work with refugees. I'm sure they're going to screen me or something. I walk over to the front desk. There's a smiling Asian woman with extremely thick, black hair, sitting there waiting for me to say something.

"Hello," I say. "My name is Hannah and I have an appointment with Marion." Why do I say it like it's a question?

"Sure," she says, but it sounds more like, shoah. "I call her. You wait. Okay?"

"Okay," I say. I bet she's a refugee. I wonder how long she's been here.

I don't have to wait long because the next thing I know, a powerful-looking gray-haired woman is coming toward me at a rapid pace. Suddenly a hand is reaching out to grab mine and I'm shaking it vigorously.

"Hannah, so good to meet you. I'm Marion."

"Hi, Marion. I'm glad to meet you, too."

"Come into my office," she says and quickly turns and starts heading away from me. I follow right behind her. I like this woman. She knows where she's going, that's for sure.

She sits at her big desk, which is piled with papers, and offers me the chair right across from it. As soon as I sit down, her face is halfway across her desk and she's smiling at me.

"I was thrilled to receive your call, Hannah. We don't get a lot of volunteers your age, as you can imagine. We need someone with lots of energy to help these families. They are very needy. Tell me again how you came to call."

I tell her the whole story even though I already told her when I first called and as I'm talking she's rummaging through her file cabinet. She pulls out a file folder and plops it down on the desk. I know what's in there. I want to grab it, but I restrain myself and wait until she offers it to me.

"Hannah, as I told you, there are several families in the Pelham Parkway section of the Bronx. Do you know the Bronx at all?"

"I've been to the zoo." Oh, sound stupid right off the bat, why don't you?

"As a matter of fact, this area is only one or two exits north of the zoo, so that's a great landmark."

"Great," I say, suddenly feeling not so stupid after all. "Then it shouldn't be too hard for me to find the place."

"First of all Hannah, what do you have in mind? I mean, as a volunteer."

"Well, I thought I'd just kind of be friends with them. And I've already got about twelve bags filled with all kinds of stuff I'm sure they'll need, so I'd like to give out what I've collected."

"You'll be their very first Santa Claus!"

I'm not sure what to say to that, so I just smile.

"Being friends is a good start, a great start. They need a friend desperately. You have no idea what these people have gone through to get here."

I tell Marion that I've read a lot about the war and the culture. As much as I could get my hands on.

"That's marvelous. Besides the essentials, I really can't tell you what they'll need. You'll just have to play it by ear. Have you considered what kind of time you have available to give them?

I hadn't really thought about it, but I say, "I was thinking of, like you said, playing it by ear. Start off by going on Saturdays, and see what happens."

"That sounds great. Just remember, if you really take this on, you'll become an integral part of their lives, so if you find this is not for you after a few tries, please don't feel obligated to continue. It will be harder for them if you say you'll show up and you don't, rather than not coming at all. After what they've been through, trust is a big issue." She gives me one of those considering looks, not really judgmental, but her look tells me not to mess with her or them. I look right back into those strong blue eyes, answering. Something shifts in her face and she's smiling again, hard.

"I know you're going to be great! I can feel it. I'm never wrong about my volunteers! Now, would you like to know something about the people you'll be working with?"

This is what I've been waiting for. I'm nodding enthusiastically. She opens the file folder that she threw on her desk. She shows me some Xeroxed copies of passport photos, so I can see what they look like. Mostly, they look sad. Many families are already here, having arrived several weeks to two months ago. There really hasn't been anyone to help them except the people at IRC, and they're so busy, no one has time to check on them. The refugees come into the office once or twice a week to check in with Marion or the other caseworkers they're assigned to. But like Marion said, my job is to be their friend.

They are all ethnic Chinese. One is a family consisting of a husband and wife with a tiny baby, born at a refugee camp in Thailand. The husband is working at a factory somewhere in New York, so the wife's alone all day. Marion doesn't know whether she's gotten to know the others living in that building, but she'd like her to. That, it seems, will be one of my jobs. Getting them together.

So I ask, "How am I going to do that when none of them speaks a word of English?"

"That's the fun part!" And that's all she says, handing me a Vietnamese/English dictionary.

These five families live either in the same building or in another nearby. There are lots of kids and Marion just picked up a family of three at the airport. They consist of a nineteen-year-old woman, her fourteen-year-old brother and four-year-old sister.

"You mean they came alone?"

"Oh, yes, Hannah. Families must separate in order to get out safely. And many of them don't make it. These three are very lucky to have survived pirates and stormy seas, not to mention the unsanitary conditions of the boat and the camps."

"Pirates?" I heard something about it on the news but I thought the newscaster must have been exaggerating. I can't believe there are still pirates in the world. The only pirates I've ever pictured are the Captain Hook type, with eye patches and bandanas on their heads, saying "Aaarh, maties." I wish it were so.

"It's terrible. Horrible! These cruel men go after refugee vessels, steal what little the people have and then rape as many women as they can. Many girls jump overboard to avoid the shame and humiliation. The pirates don't usually leave too many alive after they've done their damage. Am I shocking you?" I guess she sees my face go pale.

"Well, I guess I didn't realize."

"There's a lot the news doesn't tell us. Are you still game?"

Not only am I game, I am even more determined to do something to make their new lives here as happy as possible. I am wiping away some tears as I say, "Oh, yeah."

"Great!"

She hands me my folder and grabs my hand with both of hers. I grab them back. She tells me she will have someone call the families and let them know I'll be coming.

"When do you want to start?"

"Is this Saturday too soon?"

Mei

Chapter 44

Life is difficult here. I am afraid to walk alone on the streets and I must walk every morning to take my brother to his school. He is still not yet comfortable going alone. I grip Linh tightly as we go, our heads down against the winter chill. After we drop Tuan off, we walk back to our apartment and all the way I am in constant fear. I know it is irrational, but so it is. I look behind me, my heart racing at every stranger who approaches. Linh seems more curious than fearful and I try not to let her see my anxiety. No one has paid me the slightest mind, yet I am filled with fear that I will be robbed or worse.

I take my food stamps into the small grocery and buy some rice and some vegetables. I feel ashamed that I must use these. I want to pay with money like everyone else. I feel people are looking at me with disdain as I pull out my scrip.

Marion has helped me to find work, and though I am grateful, it is nothing I care to do. I sit all day in the same spot, putting caps onto bottles. There is no joy, no color, nothing of beauty that I can see in the drab place where I spend my day. They could not hire me to work every day, and though we are in dire need of money, I do not think I could bear this tedium daily. So I work only three days per week while my brother is at school. Marion told me that the American government will help us until I can find something full time. When I have adjusted. I hope that will be soon. Marion made sure that my boss knew that I must leave at an early hour so I can meet my brother at his school. I must be there for my siblings, always. I made that promise to my mother.

There is only one other Vietnamese working in the factory and it is an older man, so I have not found a friend. Hoang Lan, my neighbor on the first floor, is kind and friendly, but we have little in common. She has consented to care for Linh while I am working. It will be good for both Linh and Lan's little daughter, Phun. It is good of Hoang Lan to help us, for it is frightening to think of leaving Linh with anyone she does not know; though we do not know the family well, they seem kind and their child seems happy, so I must trust that Linh will be fine. I pay Hoang Lan a small amount which she readily accepts.

Though Hoang Lan and her husband have promised to do so, they have yet to accompany us to Chinatown, and I am longing to go there. Of course it has only been three weeks since we have arrived. There will be time for excursions.

We are the first family in this building to have a telephone installed. It is tan in color and has buttons rather than a dial.

Linh likes to press the buttons, but I stop her because I am afraid she will call somewhere far away and we have little money to pay for that.

I try to call my home in Vietnam, my anticipation great, my hands shaking as I press the buttons. I hear the operator in Vietnamese saying that the number is no longer in service. I feel the blood rush from my body and I am overwhelmed with despair. Tears spring to my eyes and though I want to hide them, I cannot and let them come freely. I am desperate to speak with someone from my family; to know who has left the country and who remains. I fear for their safety and want to tell them where we are and that we are well. Tomorrow I will send a telegram to my parents and pray to Kuan Yin that they receive it. I never finished my letter to them. It was stained with tears.

There is a knock on the door. My fear returns and I tentatively walk to it. "Who is it?" I peer through the tiny hole in the door but it is so distorted I cannot tell.

"It is Lan. Hoang Lan. May I come in? I have some wonderful news."

I breathe a sigh and unlock the door. Lan and her daughter, Phun, enter and I am glad for the distraction. Linh immediately takes little Phun by the hand and they go into the next room and happily play as though they are old friends. Linh loves taking on a mothering role. It is good for her.

I make tea for my neighbor who tells me that this Saturday we are to have a visitor; a volunteer who is willing to help us. Lan has been asked by Marion to tell all the others who live here.

"Here is her name." Lan hands me a slip of paper with the

name written in English. Hannah. Easy, similar to a name from my country. I try to pronounce it to myself.

"All Marion said was that she was young and energetic."

"Youth and energy are always good. I just hope we will be able to understand one another," I say to Lan, doubtfully.

"Oh, Marion did not say anything about understanding each other. Only about her youth. I doubt she speaks Vietnamese. She is American, as far as I know."

"Well, I hope she will be kind and maybe help us understand some of the ways of this strange country."

"I hope that as well."

We talk for some time, drink our tea, and then Lan takes her baby, who is reluctant to leave Linh's company, by the hand and they go home. Linh comes and climbs onto my lap and I tell her the good news. She has no idea what I am talking about, but she smiles at me anyway. My brother, who has been in his room studying English, emerges and I tell him as well. He thinks it is good news and we light a stick of incense in gratitude. We have prayed to Kuan Yin for this.

Hannah

Chapter 45

Today is Saturday. The Saturday that I'm supposed to go to the Bronx and I'm having second thoughts. What if I fail? What if we can't understand each other? Am I crazy to be doing this?

My mother is lecturing me on where to park the car, to make sure I lock it, to get out of there before dark. The Bronx is a dangerous place. My father is asking for the third time if I want him to come along, at least for the first time. He could wait in the car. I tell him no, thank you, I've got to do this myself (that is, if I do it at all).

I get the directions and put them into my Save-A-Tree bag that I use as a purse. I've got my wallet with some money my dad gave me. I filled my tank yesterday. Gas was up to $.89 a gallon, and my car has a sixteen gallon tank.

I've been trying to eat lately, but this morning I definitely can't eat breakfast, I'm so nervous. I can't turn back now; I can't leave them in the lurch. They're expecting me, that's what Marion said when I called her yesterday.

"Oh, Hannah, so glad you called. We've given your name to Hoang Lan, she's the one I told you about, with the baby. She said she's going to tell the other families."

She hears my silent gulp.

"You'll be great, I just know it. They are lovely people. You have nothing to worry about. Just have fun."

So you see there's no way I can back out now. My dad is helping me get a couple of the big, black garbage bags into the car. I don't want to overwhelm them, so I'm bringing two today. The ones with the dishes and curtains and household items. I separated the stuff according to what I thought they would need first. I hope I did it right.

I pull the directions out of my bag and place them on the seat next to me. I've never driven this far before alone, and never on a highway. The Bronx River Parkway isn't that big of a highway, but it's curvy and always seems fast when my father drives it. I'll stay in the right lane the whole time.

My mother gives me a kiss and tells me again to be careful. I tell her of course I will. My father watches as I pull slowly out of the driveway. He's just standing there, arms folded across his chest, but he isn't shaking his head. His look is different; kind of soft and nice, maybe even proud. He stands there until I can't see him from my rear view mirror. I wonder what he's thinking as he stands there, watching.

It doesn't take me too long to get on the parkway, and I'm kind of wishing it was a three hour drive. I still don't know if I'm ready for this, but I'm headed south and there's no way

I'm turning around now. From the entrance to the parkway, it only takes twenty minutes until I see the "Welcome to The Bronx" sign. My exit is coming up and my heart starts to race.

It's like entering an entirely different world as I turn onto my exit. No more houses or lawns, but brown buildings with laundry hanging out of windows even though it's freezing, kids playing in small parks that seem to be on every corner, mothers pushing bundled babies in strollers, teenagers throwing basketballs, and people, lots of them, walking in the streets. This is not suburbia.

I glance over to the piece of paper next to me and try to find my way and whether I like it or not, it's easy and I'm there in a few minutes. Naturally, there's a place to park right in front of the building and I sit for a few minutes, composing myself, looking into the mirror, a forced smile on my face. I want to see how I'll look when they see me. It just looks fake.

Forget it, whatever happens will happen. I've got to get out of the car, they're waiting for me. I wonder what Marion told them. I forgot to ask her. I wonder if they asked why some teenage American girl wants to meet them.

Apartment 1B. I'm about to ring the entrance bell when some guy opens the door from the inside and I go in.

It's really warm and steamy in the hall and it smells like fish and detergent. I can barely hear my own footsteps; my heart is beating like a drum. I find my way to 1B and I stand there stupidly for a moment. Then I knock, timidly at first and then bolder. The door opens and I have to look down. There is a tiny Vietnamese girl peeking out from under the chain. She is adorable. She looks up at me with a frightened look and closes the door shut. Great first impression. I instill fear. I contemplate running down the hall and out of here, but I raise my hand to knock once more and before I do, the door opens again. It's the same little girl, only this time she has a piece of paper in her hand. She's holding up the paper and it's got my name on it.

I bend down to tell her, "Yes, it's me!" I say pointing to myself and smiling, only this time, my smile is for real. I'm sure she has no idea what I am saying, but she smiles back at me. Her teeth are black and rotten, but her face is lit up. Someone is behind her unchaining the lock and I am let in. A young woman picks up the tiny child with the paper and takes it out of her hand and hands it to me.

"Yes, I'm Hannah. That's me!" I say pointing to the blue words on the crumpled slip and then to myself.

Her face lights into a smile and I can tell she's relieved. She would be pretty if her teeth were better. She invites me into the apartment, using gestures, not words. I wonder if any of them speak any English at all.

The apartment is bare except for a table and an easy chair showing years of use and I silently count eleven people sitting on the floor. Four of them are women, all looking shrunken and old, even though I know they are still young. They are skinny and all dressed in what looks like silk pajamas. I am so nervous I can barely breathe, and they seem as nervous as I am. I can see in their look that they do not know what to make of me. Marion said that trust is a big issue for them and after knowing what I know about how they got here, I can understand why. They are looking at me with something between bewilderment and fear, but the woman who opened the door for me touches me lightly on my arm and makes a welcoming gesture, offering me the one chair. There are two men on the floor looking at me with a combination of suspicion and, could it be, amusement? They also gesture for me to sit down in the chair, but I shake my head and sit myself down on the floor with them.

I can tell by the way they shift and smile slightly they are pleased by this. The woman who greeted me mimes someone drinking out of a cup, and shuffles into the kitchen where I assume she's going to make tea.

I'm not sure what to do now, with the hostess gone. No one says a word. I think I'm shaking. Be brave Hannah, I tell myself. You wanted to do this! I take a breath, probably too loudly, and start talking. First I point to myself and tell them my name. "I'm Hannah, Haaa - naahhh," I say, making it easy for them to pronounce. They each repeat my name over and over as if it is a precious thing. "And yours?" I gesture to them to tell me theirs. They seem to understand and they take turns, each saying a name that sounds strange to my American ears and each one harder for me to pronounce than the next. I can tell they're pleased that I am trying to say them properly. I can also tell by their smiles that I'm butchering them. I begin to relax a little.

We sit for a while this way, them saying their names, me butchering. It almost becomes a game. By the end of it, we're all smiling.

The children are sitting on the other side of me and after I get through practicing all the adult names, I turn to them. I smile my warmest smile at them. I don't think I've smiled this much in a really long time, but it feels natural here. They just stare at me until the little girl who had first opened the door smiles again and the rest follow. I'm thinking about what I've read in the files Marion gave me about these people. It's incredible that these kids are still able to smile after what they've seen and been through. I am amazed. I want to reach out and hug every one of them and in that moment, it feels like my heart is cracking open. It's like finding something wonderful hidden in an ugly box. Tears spring to my eyes and I immediately pretend to cough so I can wipe them away.

Besides the little girl who greeted me, there is a teenage boy a few years younger than I, a small girl of about four and two toddlers. After the initial ice is broken, it becomes slightly awkward again until one of the women gets up and calls to her tiny daughter. She tells her something in Vietnamese and the girl stands in front of me and begins to whistle. She is about two at the most, and I'm thinking it's got to be the most adorable thing I've ever seen in my life. I clap my hands and laugh and they all laugh with me as she takes a little bow.

Not to be outdone, the other baby, a boy of about the same age, stands in front of us giggling, and proceeds to pee on the floor. His mother smiles at me, embarrassed, half bows and quickly wipes up the spill with a rag that seems to have been used for that purpose before. We all laugh and I feel much more relaxed, but even weirder, I feel at home.

I am served tea in a chipped cup, and there are leaves floating in it. There are only a limited amount of cups, so I wait until someone else sips theirs, then I do. The tea is strong and slightly nutty, a little bitter. I have a little trouble drinking through the floating leaves and hope I don't have any leaves stuck to my teeth, but I drink it all, every drop.

I pull my Vietnamese/English dictionary out of my bag

and our attempts to talk to each other become like a game and the tension that was so present when I first got here slips further away. I tell them I am seventeen years old.

"Tôi muoi bay," I say, wondering how to pronounce all the accent marks and strange dots on top of the letters. What I actually said or tried to say was "I seventeen." I ask them what they need. I do this by pointing and saying "Nhu câu?" Need?

The young woman, Phoung Mei, who arrived with the brother and sister, gestures for me to show her the book and point to the word. Obviously they have no idea what I just asked. She smiles and shakes her head, then says it correctly. Boy was I off. And so it begins. I look up a word and show it to Mei, she pronounces it, I repeat. She answers by looking her word up in the Vietnamese section, pointing to it, and I pronounce the English, which she repeats. I find out that they really need everything. IRC gave them the basics to get started, but they need so much more. More tea cups to begin with.

"Màn cua sô," she says, pointing to the word for curtains and I repeat. She nods approvingly. Then I say, "curtains," and she tries to repeat that. We do this for several more things they need; shoes - giày, scissors – kéo, needle and thread – kim and soi…

I think I might have some of those things in the car. I can't figure out how to tell them all this information, so I pull out a pad and pen and begin to draw a car with bags, with a teapot sticking out of a bag. It's a pathetic attempt, but it works. I get up and pantomime what I need to do, putting on my coat. The teenage boy, Tuan, gives me the wait signal and he leaves the apartment. He's back in three minutes with his coat on (which happens to be enormous) and together we go out to get the bags.

Meí

Chapter 46

What a strange girl who has come to call on us! She sits right down on the floor with us, crossing her legs as easily as any Buddhist! She tries to speak our language, although she makes it sound ridiculous, but nevertheless, she tries. And so skinny! I thought Americans were all supposed to be fat, but this one, why she is as skinny as I am. And young! How can someone so young want to help people she has never met and knows nothing about? I thought all American teenagers were supposed to be selfish, listening to rock and roll and disrespecting authority. Oh, what misconceptions!

This girl, Hannah, has put us at ease, even the men, who were so suspicious. She tells us, using her dictionary, that she is seventeen, a high school student. As young as my third brother, younger than my second sister! I do not think she is here by force; her smile makes us know that she genuinely wants to be. And how it makes her face look so gaunt!

There is something about this girl that makes me feel that we are kindred spirits, and for the life of me, I cannot say why. But without even thinking, I tell her I want curtains! How presumptuous of me! I am ashamed of my behavior. Of course we have no idea what she is saying, but she is smart and she draws pictures so we can understand one another. Her drawings are so childish, but sweet somehow. I long to take the pen from her and sketch all the things we need. It would be a lot easier than all this pointing and repeating. But it has given us a way to communicate and I need to learn English. And it has been too long since I have drawn even the smallest thing.

My brother follows her out into the cold and together they bring back two large plastic bags. She sits on the floor with her bags in front of her and to my complete surprise, little Linh, my shy sister, sidles up next to her. Right next to her! Hannah looks somewhat shocked and pleased and she ruffles my sister's hair. Together, the two of them begin to pull things out of the bag. She gives them to Linh, who holds them up proudly.

There are colorful bed sheets with flowers on them, pillow cases, towels, forks, spoons, knives. Linh and Hannah place them neatly on the floor and we all stare at them, all wanting to grab at these valuables, none of us daring to make the first move. I want the colorful sheets, but I will wait for the curtains to be pulled out and hope they are as nice. I know we are all somewhat ashamed that we must take used items from a plastic bag when before, many of us could give to charity; we could sleep on the finest linens. But circumstances have changed and we must accept our lot. And instead of making us feel like beggars, this girl makes us feel as though these are gifts just for us!

Hannah is smiling as she pulls out the faded curtains. They are pale yellow with tiny violet flowers on them. She does not put them on the floor with the other things, but hands them directly to me. She nods her head and says something. I wish I understood what she was saying, but her meaning is clear. "These are for you. I hope you like them." And I do. They are perfect. I ask for her dictionary and look up the word, dep – lovely, I tell her. Câm on - thank you.

She stands up and takes them from me and holds them up. They will be just the right length for my windows. I will need to buy the rods to go with them. But no, to my delight, she pulls those out of the bag as well! Linh claps her hands!

"Thank you, Hannah," I say in my bad English.

"You are welcome!" she replies, slowly so that I can try to understand her.

This has put everyone at ease and then it is a happy free for all as we take what we need, trade for what we want and when we are all done, there is no one who is bitter, no one who wants what someone else has. Hannah asks for a list of what else we might need and everyone freely tells her. She manages to tell us that she has many more bags at her home and will bring them next week. I like the sound of that – next week. "Tuân sau." This means she will return.

Hoang Lan is requesting that Hannah stay for dinner, but I can tell that the poor girl has no idea what Lan is saying. I tell my brother to try to translate. The fact that he can speak enough English to help after such a short time makes me feel as proud as any mother.

"Hannah," Tuan says awkwardly, "You eat here?"

Hannah looks at her watch, but we are all surrounding her, none of us wanting her to go. She looks at each of us, her eyes lingering on Linh, her smile softening when my sister returns the smile, and she nods her head. We will make her a Vietnamese meal to thank her for all she has done for us this day. I hope she likes it.

Hannah

Chapter 47

What a day! I can hardly believe this feeling I have. It's almost embarrassing! I haven't smiled this much since I was maybe nine! I feel like something has cracked open inside me and I want to stay here and bask in this feeling. These people are so kind and they're so grateful for even the smallest thing. It makes me feel guilty for every time I ever whined about wanting something I truly didn't need.

I give Mei the curtains, the ones I got from the temple donations. I'd better stop complaining about the rich establishment. If they weren't so rich they never would have gotten rid of such nice curtains. The smile on her face when I hand them to her is enough to make me feel like I did something great today! And now they're asking me to stay for dinner! I wasn't expecting this. Not yet. But I'm definitely going to stay.

They are all very nice, but the family of three, the Phoung family; Mei, Linh and Tuan are the ones I immediately feel drawn to. Especially Mei. I think we are going to be friends. And Linh! She is absolutely adorable. She's got this pitch black hair cut straight to her shoulders with straight bangs across her black eyes. She's very serious, but when she smiles her whole face lights up!

I wish I could communicate with them. The only one who seems to know any English at all is Tuan, but he's quite shy. And I'm sure my attempt at Vietnamese is pathetic, but we seem to understand each other and that's all that counts for now.

People who had left the apartment a while ago are coming back in with covered pots and dishes, and the smells coming from the kitchen are pungent and mouthwatering. I have never eaten Vietnamese food before and I'm kind of nervous, but I love Chinese food so much, I doubt it's all that different. Mei delivers something to the kitchen and then she comes back out to try and talk with me.

"Hannah, when day you back?" she says and I can tell she's really embarrassed. Her cheeks turn bright red.

I want her to feel safe to try to speak in front of me, so I say, "Good! You must have learned some English in the camps. I'll come back next Saturday. Sa-tur-day." I notice a big calendar hanging from the wall, the kind I've seen in Chinese restaurants, only this one has Vietnamese writing on it. There's a picture of a pretty Vietnamese woman in front of a seriously fake view of some rice paddies. I point to next Saturday.

"Saturday," I repeat.

"Saturday," she repeats. Her accent is so thick.

"Sunday, Monday, Tuesday, Wednesday, Thursday, Friday, Saturday," I say while pointing to the days in Vietnamese that I assume are in the same order. Mei points to Sunday and I say it again. She says it after me. So do Linh and Tuan. Then we go to Monday. A couple more people come out of the kitchen and so starts my first English class.

By the time dinner is ready, everybody except Hoang Lan (who is still cooking) is sitting at the table or on the floor listening and repeating. I've taught them the days of the week, months of the year and numbers to thirty one.

Hoang Lan brings in a huge bowl of steaming white rice and I am placed at the head of the table. Mei and another woman, Nhung, go into the kitchen to help bring out the dishes. And we are having a feast. I feel somewhat ashamed as I'm sure they're using their week's supply of food for this dinner, especially for me with my appetite (all but non-existent) but I'm going to eat every bite they serve me. I cannot make a fool of myself or let them know I have this stupid eating problem! Luckily they don't actually serve me, but give me a bowl of rice with a pair of chopsticks. The steaming bowls of food are all in the middle of the table, so I can take as much (or as little) as I want. But I will try everything.

"This is delicious!" I honestly say as I bite into something that looks like a sausage.

"Lap chen, good, good," one of the older men says. I don't know whether that's what it's called or if it means something. Whatever it is, I repeat it. "Lap chen! Good!"

I think I'm making a good impression. I can use chopsticks and I can tell they're impressed about that! Plus, I'm actually eating everything and I really do think it's delicious! I'd eat this stuff every day if I could! There's soup with bits of chicken and vegetables floating in it. It has a spicy taste, kind of sweet and sour, too. There's a dish of noodles, some chicken pieces with the bones on them in a delicious sauce, and some kind of fish dish.

At the end of the meal, Hoang Lan grabs some used glasses and goes into the kitchen. A minute or so later, she's back out with the glasses, now clean and wet. She places them on the table, spoons sticking out of each one, and scoops instant coffee into them, pours in boiling water and then sweetened condensed milk from a can. She hands me one and stirs it for me, gesturing for me to keep stirring. I do until they tell me in Vietnamese to try it. Oh, my God is it delicious. I don't really like coffee, but this is unreal!

"Cà phê phin," Mei says, a big smile on her face as she sips hers.

"Cà phê phin," I say back, sipping mine with an equally happy grin. It'll probably keep me up all night, but who cares! I doubt I'm going to sleep a wink tonight anyway, I'm so excited.

It's late and cold when Tuan and Mei walk me to my car. I try to get them to stay inside but they insist on coming with me and they're only wearing flip-flops! But to be honest, I'm actually glad they do, especially after listening to my mother's warnings. It's after nine by the time I'm heading North on the Bronx River Parkway. I didn't even call my parents. They're probably freaking out. I've been gone for hours! And I wish I could have stayed longer.

Meí

Chapter 48

I wait on line in this welfare office, trying to hide my face from the shame of it. Each time I come here there is some kind of turmoil, someone yelling, a fight. It frightens me and I wish I could find a good job so that I would not have to take money from the government. The welfare workers are not unfriendly, but are very brusque and my smiles are never reciprocated. They ask me questions that I have trouble understanding. I tell them I am studying English and looking for a better job. This seems to satisfy them and they print out a check for me.

I brought Tuan with me when I first came, forcing him to leave school early so that he could accompany me. This is unfair to him, so these days I come alone. After I receive my check, I put it carefully in my pouch, the one I made at the camp, and walk quickly back to the subway and home. I am on my guard at all times and silently utter the name of Kuan Yin for the entire ride to my stop. I look at no one on these rides. I am sure I seem unfriendly.

The local grocer will cash the check for me as long as I buy goods from him, and so I do. Today I buy pork and onions so that I can make Canh bi Dao, a special and delicious soup I will serve my brother and sister. I have good news to tell them.

I finally received a telegram from my parents. They are still in our house, though everything inside (including the telephone) was taken from us, but everyone is safe and that is good news. I was afraid my father would be taken to a re-education camp, but so far this has not happened. Three more of my siblings have left the country and have the information I telegrammed them when we arrived here. This makes me breathe a sigh of relief, knowing they know where to find me. My sixteen-year-old brother, Hien, and my sisters, Cam, age eleven, and Nhung, age nine, were the ones to leave after us. My parents do not know where they are at this time, but hope they are safe. I hope this too and hope they are able to contact me soon. I am desperate to reunite with my family.

I serve the soup and Tuan looks at me with expectation. He knows this soup is for special occasions. I tell Tuan and Linh that I have heard from our parents and that three more of our siblings are on their way. Tuan shouts with joy and Linh claps her hands together. We slurp our soup happily.

When I visit Marion the next day I tell her (through Danh) my good news. I ask her to help me find a better job so I can get more money to help my family. She looks through some papers and finds one job in Manhattan, working in a hotel, cleaning the rooms. The hours are many and I am not sure I want to leave Linh with Hoang Lan for so long. I am not even sure Hoang Lan would be willing to take her for so much more time, though Linh is such a good and sweet child and no trouble to anyone. I will think about this. I wish I had enough English to ask Hannah her opinion. I will ask her when she comes on Saturday.

We are all beginning to trust her. Because of Hannah, we all have gotten to know each other. She has been here five weeks in a row; every Saturday she comes, bringing gifts in those big black bags, teaching us English, playing with the little ones, especially Linh. She and Linh are becoming fast friends. Linh seems to have taken to Hannah unlike I have seen her take to anyone. Whenever Hannah arrives, my little sister runs up to her and immediately begins tickling her and wants to be tickled by her. I am happy that Linh can feel such love for someone. I was worried for her after we left our mother. I knew she was angry and thought perhaps she could only love me, but I am glad to see this is not so. And Hannah seems pleased by her affection.

And now, these Saturday evening dinners are becoming ritual. We ask her to stay and she happily accepts.

We are all feeling less afraid and more confident since she has come. We have an American friend and this means a lot. Hannah has given us her telephone number and told us we may call her anytime we need help. She tells us she lives only twenty five minutes from here and would come anytime we need her. Of course, we would never think to bother her, but knowing she is near has made us feel a little more secure. And now that it is a little warmer, Hannah has promised to bring us to Chinatown.

This Saturday, dinner is a happy affair, for when I try to tell Hannah my news, it seems I have said it correctly and she understands. Everyone cheers. We all eat with gusto and it seems that Hannah has taken a liking to our cuisine and wants to know the names of everything we are eating. We help her pronounce the names of the dishes in Vietnamese and Chinese and surprisingly, her pronunciation is excellent. And she continues to teach us English. After dinner we sit and drink cà phê phin or tea and she walks around the room pointing to objects, telling us their English name, waiting for us to repeat them. Sometimes we repeat them in unison, other times she asks us to say them alone. We adults do not seem to have the knack for it and we are somewhat embarrassed to speak aloud, but the younger ones! They repeat each word she says without a trace of shyness. And they love to play games with Hannah. Last week she brought cards to play, a way of teaching the children numbers, and they played for hours. Then we taught Hannah a Vietnamese card game. Tonight she pulls out the cards and asks if we would like to play. I never would have thought being in this strange new country would be as enjoyable as it is. I wonder if other refugees are lucky enough to have someone like Hannah befriending them.

She has taught the little ones children's songs, which they sing all day long. I have gotten some of those songs stuck in my head. I think that is a good thing.

Tonight, after the card game, before she is ready to return to her home, I ask her to come to our apartment and proudly show her my curtains, the ones she gave to me. I want to say thank you and I do. She smiles and touches my shoulder. "You are very welcome," she says, and this time I understand.

Hannah

Chapter 49

I love this! I can't believe what fun I'm having! I cannot wait for Saturdays now when I get into my car and drive to the Bronx! And how great it is to have all these new friends, because really, that's what they are. Especially Mei, Tuan and Linh. Every time I come over Linh wants to play what I call the "ticklik" game. That's how she says "tickle," "ticklik." It's adorable. She chases me around the apartment trying to tickle me. The other little ones always join in and it's a free-for-all. The parents don't seem to mind, and it's not like the apartment has anything breakable or lots of furniture to bump into. I think the parents are actually relieved. I'm kind of like a baby-sitter when I come, and I don't mind at all. I like this kind of baby-sitting! I'm teaching the little kids English and they're learning way faster than the adults. They are so cute when they speak English with their thick Vietnamese accents.

I wonder if the little ones will lose their accents. I doubt the adults will.

I can't believe what happened last week. I had grabbed three big black bags from our back porch to bring to the families. I hauled them up with Tuan's help (he always helps me) and I opened the first one. Mostly clothes and shoes. I dumped it out and everyone looked for what they needed. Then I opened the second one and I was assaulted with a terrible smell coming out of it. Oh, my God! I realized I had brought our garbage! I was so embarrassed I could hardly stand it. I'm sure I gasped. I closed it up tight and ran to put it outside the door. Then I peeked into the next bag. Same thing!

I put my hand in front of my mouth and I'm sure I must have turned every shade of red imaginable. I was hoping they didn't understand what was going on, but then they all started laughing. I mean really laughing. Not maliciously or anything, but to try to make me feel better. It was kind of funny, I guess. I started laughing, too, and asked how to say, "I'm so embarrassed."

"Bu hao yi suh!" Tuan told me. "That's Chinese," he said. "Very good expression."

I sure was bu hao yi suh! But they weren't mad at all. I made sure to look into the bags I brought today!

I haven't brought my camera because I didn't think it would be appropriate until I got to know them better, but I think I'm gonna bring it next week. Of course I'll ask permission first. I know in some cultures people believe their soul is taken when someone takes their picture. I will be respectful of their culture even though I'm dying to take some pictures. I want to take everyone's, but I'm thinking if I start with the kids, the adults will be okay with it. They'll love it if I bring them copies of what I shoot. And the kids are so cute.

They're definitely beginning to trust me and I think they look forward to my visits. I always ask them before I leave if they are busy next week and should I come. It's always an enthusiastic yes.

Next week I'm taking them to Chinatown by subway. Gulp. But I've got a subway map and it's pretty straightforward. I wonder if they would find it weird if they knew my relationship to Chinatown. But they're Buddhists, so I bet they believe in reincarnation. We haven't had that discussion yet, their English isn't up to it, and neither is my Vietnamese. I'd love to ask them about it. Hoang Lan has a little red altar with incense and fruit. So does Mei. I've actually only been inside those two apartments, but I'm sure they all have them. They asked me if I believe in Jesus like most Americans. I was a little nervous telling them no, I'm Jewish. I never know what people will say when I tell them. Will they give me a dirty look, call me 'kike,' like some kids at school used to, or accept me as I am?

I looked it up in my Vietnamese dictionary and showed them the word. They nodded. That's it. That's good I guess. They still want me to come back.

Tonight Mei asks me to come up to her apartment and after I say goodbye to everyone, I go upstairs with her, Tuan and Linh. She shows me her curtains hanging from her windows. They look great and I tell her so.

"Thank you, Hannah," she says really slowly and carefully.

"You are very welcome," I tell her.

I don't know why, but I get this idea. "Do you have any tape?" I ask Tuan who understands the most and I do a little pantomime.

"Yes, Hannah." He goes into the kitchen and gets me some. I have some paper in my bag. I take it out and fold it into small squares. I try to rip it evenly. On each square I write a word for an object in their apartment. I write 'door' and take a piece of tape and nod for permission and then tape it to the door. The three of them are following me around the apartment and we are getting more excited by the minute. When I'm done, I've labeled window, stove, sink, refrigerator, counter, toilet, mirror, table, chair, and telephone. I know I could do more, but this is enough for tonight. Mei takes my hand and thanks me again. I hold back tears. Why am I crying? They're the ones who've lost everything. I take her hand and smile. I better not speak or I'll lose it. Linh puts her small arms around my legs and I pick her up. "See you next week, okay?"

"Okay," she replies.

Before I leave, Tuan comes to me and shows me a math worksheet that he has brought home. It's riddled with red marks and a big 'F'. The teacher wrote this comment,

"What is the meaning of this!"

"Hannah, this no good, yes? I not understand this problems," Tuan says, really upset and confused. He pulls out some more math papers from his binder and again, red marks. I am shaking my head, (oh my God, like my father) but I'm so mad. Does his teacher have any idea who she is teaching?

"Don't worry, Tuan, I'll talk with your teacher," I say really slowly.

"You do, Hannah? Thank you. I want do good in school. Not bad like this."

I decide that I'm cutting fourth period on Monday to pay his teacher a visit. I can tell he is truly confused as to why she would grade him so unsympathetically. When I ask him if he has a special class for English, he looks at me in confusion.

"No special class, Hannah. I am try to learn, but teacher speak too quickly."

"I'll be there on Monday," I tell him. He gives me this relieved smile and I know it's what I've got to do. I'll try to behave. I wouldn't want his teacher to have it in for him because I'm so mad. I'll pretend I'm his social worker. I'll be polite.

Mei

Chapter 50

There is an English class at a Jewish place of worship near our apartment and Hannah encourages me to attend. There are mostly Russian people in the beginner class, but now a few Vietnamese have joined. I have gone to four classes and the teacher, a nice older woman, gives me two books to study from; Side by Side. I have a textbook and a workbook. Every night I study the textbook and I write in my workbook. The class is held twice per week and I will try to go to each one. The place is very near our building and Tuan is old enough to stay with Linh for a few hours. I make sure he locks the door as soon as I leave and when I return, I have a special knock that tells him it is me at the door. He tells me not to worry so much and to study hard. He is such a good brother.

There are about fifteen people in the class. The Russians seem very determined about learning English and they speak up in class often. The teacher tries to get us all to speak up, but we Vietnamese are so shy. We avoid each other's eyes and practically whisper our answers. Our teacher tries to encourage us and I wonder what trauma prevents us from voicing even the simplest greeting or question. How can the Russians be so bold and we so meek? I will try to speak loudly and have courage. How will I ever communicate with my new friend if I am too shy to learn her language, the language of my new country? I have heard of people who came here many years ago and who still cannot speak the language. I find it absurd. To rely on others to shop for you, ask questions, get information and to never get to know the people who live here! No, I will learn English, I promise myself. I will try harder. I will participate in class. I must.

I met a nice Vietnamese woman named Pham Da'o. She is about my age and lives only a few blocks from here. She came with her auntie and cousin. Her parents and two brothers were killed by the Vietcong. She tells me she has bad dreams every night. When she tells me this, I am silent, but I too have bad dreams.

I have told no one about my dreams, but they started coming soon after we arrived. They wake me up in the darkest hours of the night. Sometimes I forget where I am when I wake up bathed in cold sweat breathing hard. I look up at the cracked ceiling, so different from the thatch in the camp or the metal shingles and wooden crossbeams of our house, and I remember I am in New York, the Bronx. Far, far from my home.

My dreams are never exactly the same, but the threads of them weave together and they are all about my journey here.

Boats in swells, wormy rice, boys crying blood, men in uniform with harsh voices, my father on his knees, my mother clutching the air, my paints lying in their grave beneath the wisteria.

I look over at Linh, breathing softly, sleeping peacefully and I envy her. Does she not remember what we saw? What we experienced? Or does she live only now, as we are taught to do in our philosophy? I would like to try to live in the moment, but too much past creeps into my psyche. I really do not want to forget. And I know I never will. My experiences will mold me and shape me. I wish, though, I could choose what I dream about.

Hannah

Chapter 51

I arrive early today and everybody is ready and waiting when I ring the bell. They've got eager faces and empty cloth bags ready to fill. I am taking them to Chinatown. Some have already been, but Mei, Tuan and Linh have not, and I can tell they're excited. Linh is even jumping up and down, grabbing my hand.

Tuan is all smiles, his shyness with me entirely gone. I think I really won him over when I went to his school and advocated for him. I met his math teacher during her break time and brought his math papers with me. I asked her why she gave him these marks and why she wrote such awful comments. She said, "Just look at the work and you should be able to see why!" I asked her if she knew anything about this boy. She said she didn't. I told her he was a refugee from Vietnam, a Boat Person, that he didn't speak English, that he'd probably been through hell, and there were more of his family coming. You should have seen her face change. She said she had no idea, that she was sorry and she'd work with him, help him. I didn't use my nasty tone with her. I was really mature. I hope she keeps her word.

My sister, Ruthie, asked if she could come with me today, and I actually let her. I could tell my parents were happy about it. She is standing in the doorway looking very shy, but I drag her inside and everyone makes her feel welcome.

"Look you, Hannah," Lan says, smiling at my sister. Does she really look like me? I look over to Ruthie who probably doesn't think it's a compliment. I smile at her.

Joni was nearly hysterical that I didn't bring her, but there's no way I want to be responsible for an eight-year-old. I'm planning to invite Mei and her family to our house and I told Joni that she'd get a chance to meet them soon.

The subway ride takes a long time. First we have to get from the Bronx to Manhattan, then all the way to Canal Street. When we emerge from the subway, Tuan and Mei talk a mile a minute, pointing at Chinese signs, buildings in the shapes of pagodas, and crowds of people, all looking very much like them. I want to take them to our favorite restaurant, Ting Fu Garden, which has the best cold noodles I've ever tasted. I brought money and I want to treat them to lunch. They've treated me every time I come over! There are nine of us, and everyone has his or her own ideas of what they want to do, so we decide to meet at the subway entrance at four o'clock. Huang Lan, her husband Binh and their baby, Phun, have been here before and they take Thao Duc, one of the older men, with them. Ruthie and I stick with Mei, Tuan and Linh.

In fact, I couldn't separate from them if I wanted to because Linh has my hand in hers and has no intention of letting go of it.

We walk up Canal Street stopping every few steps to look in this window or that. We turn onto Mott Street and I'm so excited just watching them. Even my sister is excited. She knows this a big deal for them. They want to go into every shop and so we do. Mei doesn't buy anything, but just looks around, fascinated.

"Is this anything like Vietnam?" I ask.

"Like markets, yes, like Saigon," Tuan answers.

"Ho Chi Minh," Mei corrects.

I wish Mei could speak more English. I know we could become great friends if we could only talk to each other.

"Hannah, you like Chinatown?" Mei asks, like she read my mind.

"Oh, I like it very much. It's fun."

"Fun. What fun?"

How do I explain fun? I point to the colorful parasols and toys that someone is selling on the street. I pick Linh up and spin her around. "Fun!"

"Fun," she repeats.

"Do you like Chinatown?"

"Yes, I like. Thanks you, Hannah."

I don't correct her. I just smile. We window shop for another half an hour. Everywhere people are speaking Chinese loudly and excitedly. It's very festive and Tuan and Mei look more relaxed than any time I've ever seen them. They are marveling at what is sold in the shops that line the streets and talk in combinations of Chinese and Vietnamese. I guess I'm developing a good ear because I can tell the difference easily. I've decided that I want to learn one or the other. I haven't decided which, though.

We turn down Pell Street and I ask them if they're hungry. Ruthie says she is. She hasn't said much and I think she's shy because Tuan is about her age and maybe she feels awkward.

"Are you hungry, Linh?" I ask, rubbing my own belly.

She nods her head and I gesture to her brother and sister, who seem to be embarrassed. I wonder if they don't have much money, and so I tell them I want to take them to lunch. I don't know if they understand me, but I just walk ahead and they follow. I lead them into Ting Fu Garden. It's a dinky little hole-in-the-wall on Pell Street, with plastic tables and ugly wallpaper, and I almost think Mei is relieved when she sees it's anything but fancy. The waitress looks at us strangely and I wonder if she's ever seen Asians and whites together. She points to a large round table with the remnants of the previous customers' meal and so we sit. She cleans it quickly and not too thoroughly and drops some menus in front of us. Mei and Tuan hesitate, but I open mine and tell them to look at theirs. The menus are in Chinese and English, but I already know what I'm ordering: cold noodles with sesame sauce and dried, sautéed, string beans.

"Please order anything you want. I'm treating you."

"Hannah, can I have chicken with walnuts?" Ruthie asks.

"Yeah, of course!" Ruthie's looking at me strangely, as if she doesn't know me. I can almost hear her ask, so what's the catch? I guess I'm usually not this generous, and it takes her by surprise, but I'm really feeling it. It's new for me too, I must admit.

The waitress comes over and speaks to Mei in Chinese and it seems like they have an entire conversation, but the woman is writing things down on her tiny pad. She looks at me and I give her the rest of the order. I wonder what Mei ordered and I hope she likes what I did. We sit quietly for a moment, drinking the tea that Tuan has poured into our white chipped cups with pink rims.

"Hannah, you very good. People all say," Mei says hesitantly.

I'm not sure how to respond. "I'm glad," is all I can think of.

"Hannah, why you do?" I can tell Tuan is getting uncomfortable with this conversation, because he whispers something to his sister a bit hotly.

"It's all right, Tuan, I'm glad Mei asked. To tell you the truth," I say, looking at Mei, "I really don't know why. I just wanted to help and now I feel like we're friends and so I want to show you my country and what it's like here. Am I talking too fast?"

"Little," she says.

"I want to help, that's all."

The food comes and we pick up our chopsticks and eat. Mei ordered two dishes, one with tiny shrimp and cabbage and one with pork and dried tofu and some kind of green vegetable. They love what I ordered and I'm glad. Linh has a grand time picking the candied walnuts out of the chicken and crunching them for all of us to hear.

The bill comes and Mei pulls out a battered purse, but I have grabbed the check and will not let her see it. I shake my head and tell her to put her money away.

"Thank you, Hannah."

"You're welcome, my pleasure!"

We spend the rest of the day shopping. Ruthie and I are following them around, because even though we've been here tons of times, they know what they're doing, they can communicate with the shopkeepers. They even find a Vietnamese shop. I can tell because the writing is different. By the time three-thirty comes around, Mei and Tuan are laden with bags filled with bottles of fish sauce and soy sauce, cans of water chestnuts and mystery items, fresh fish, heads and all, weird looking green vegetables I've never seen before, dried mushrooms and a huge bag of rice.

As we're walking on Mulberry Street, Mei stops short in front of a shop and peers in, looking intense. I look to see what she's looking at, wondering if she recognizes someone in there, but all I see are art supplies: paints, Chinese style brushes, rice paper. She puts her hand to the window for a split second and then walks on. I wonder what that's about.

Then she sees a temple and asks to go inside. She hands me her bags and we wait. I watch as she enters the colorful pagoda-roofed building. Through the slit in the door, I see her light a stick of incense and hold it between her two hands, moving them up and down in some kind of offering. She bows her head and then she places the incense on the altar. She returns and tries to take the bags from me and I let her have a couple, but I hold on to two heavy ones. She smiles at me. The rest of the people are there on time when we arrive at Canal Street Station and we ride the Number Six together to Grand Central then change for the Bronx. Everyone seems tired but very happy, fully loaded with bag upon bag of stuff.

I don't know about anyone else, but I feel great. We don't get back until after five, and of course they insist we stay for dinner. Ruthie looks at me, hoping I'll say yes and of course I do. This night, we have a bigger feast than we've had so far, and I hope they haven't used everything they bought just for this meal.

On the ride home that night, Ruthie is still very quiet.

"Hey, Ru, you're so quiet. What's wrong?"

"Nothing's wrong. I was just thinking."

"Thinking what?"

"About not having our family, you know, if we had to be separated. I mean sometimes I hate your guts..."

"Thanks a lot," I interrupt.

"You know what I mean. I wouldn't want anything to happen to us like what happened to them. I think what Mei said was true, Hannah. What you're doing, it's good."

I don't know what to say to this. Her hand is on the seat next to me and I put my hand on it and curl my fingers around it. She curls hers back.

Mei

Chapter 52

Marion called today to tell me the news I have been waiting for. My brother and two sisters are safe in Thailand and have been approved to come to New York. They will be leaving in a few more weeks, and I will see them before a month is out! We have only been here four months and already they are coming! Kuan Yin must be watching over us! Linh drew a happy face and placed it on the altar. That will make six of us, safely together. Thank goodness for the UNHCR or we would be scattered to the winds like spiders after a storm.

Oh, I feel happy. I will make a special meal and tell Tuan the news over his favorite dish, Suon Ram. I will buy the pork ribs right away, and thank goodness we have plenty of nuoc mam, the fish sauce my brother loves so well. I bought two bottles when we went to Chinatown.

Ah, Chinatown. So full of color and sounds and smells. It almost felt like I was back in my country. I want to return to that part of New York very soon. There is so much to see and do there. I stopped at a window filled with special things just for artists. I stood, gazing longingly, wanting to stand there longer or perhaps even enter, but I dared not. I am afraid of what will come out of my hand should I lift a brush to paper. And of course, my money was only for food and those supplies we need. Perhaps my mother was right and my painting is merely a frivolity. What little money I earn must be used only for the things we need. I recall telling my parents that I needed my paints, but I have been without them so long, did I really need them at all? Perhaps like my beloved country, which can no longer be my home, I must put my painting behind me. I will pray for guidance about this.

I prayed for our family's reunification at a small temple and I am sure Kuan Yin was listening, for now my good news has come and I can breathe a little more easily. I do believe she listens.

I would like to call my friend, Hannah, and tell her my news, but my English is still so poor, though my teacher says I am making progress. I believe she tells that to all her students. We are all painfully bashful and the poor woman must work hard to get anything out of us. The Russians are bolder, but generally, we prefer to repeat in unison, and rarely venture to speak a sentence aloud, alone. Although I have almost completed all the lessons in my English book, and have been working diligently to do my homework as my teacher requires, I cannot understand much and can say even less. My brother wants to practice with me, but I am too shy and nervous.

"If you won't speak with me, Number One sister, then I have my doubts that you will speak with anyone. I will never ridicule you. Come, try a few words," Tuan says kindly, but my heart is in my mouth, even in front of my own brother.

"Come, just a few words. I'll start. 'Good evening, sister,'" he says in his heavily accented English.

I take a deep breath, "Good evening, brother, how are you?"

Tuan claps his hands. "Very good! A bit more?"

I nod my head. And smile.

Hannah

Chapter 53

School is better now that I know I'll be leaving and going to the Project. There are only a few more weeks and it's warm again, so I've started to eat outside. Sometimes Richard eats with me, but mostly it's just me. I haven't told anyone that I'm working with refugees, except Mrs. Rosenkrantz, who I now only have to see once a month. She nods her head and tells me that she's proud of me. I wonder why she says that. She really doesn't know me all that well, except to hear my complaints and problems every week. I mean, does she think about me at all after I leave her office? I don't think about her. What I do think about is what I do every Saturday and I find myself smiling at different times. It feels strange and unnatural. Sometimes I'm embarrassed by my feelings. I've been bitchy and angry for so long, it almost seems phony to feel good inside. I haven't missed one weekend since I started working with the refugees. That's nearly three months! Obviously I don't work at the library on Saturdays anymore, but when I told the supervisor why, she was okay with it. Now I work three afternoons a week.

When I tell Richard I'm leaving for my senior year to go to the Project, he seems kind of sad. I don't feel guilty or anything. I'm not going to stay for just one friend. Maybe I'll talk him into going, too. He's very artistic and eccentric, so he might fit in there. But actually, I think he's found his niche at school with the drama club. He's really good at it and he's started to write his own plays. I know he wants me to join, but there's no way. I used to want to be in the club, but my seventh grade social studies teacher who moonlighted as the drama coach would never cast me for anything no matter how many times I auditioned. He wouldn't even cast me as a stenographer who had no lines! So I gave up that dream.

My grades are decent this semester, even in math. Thank God for Mr. Lorie who never humiliates me but actually explains stuff so I can understand. I think I might even pass!

It's weird; I've been in such a good mood lately that I find myself unaffected by the girls who used to make me sick. I can walk down the hall at school and I don't care, I really don't care, when I see them whisper something as I go by, or making some comment aimed at me. Amy doesn't even bother me anymore. In fact, she passed me in the hall the other day and said hi. I couldn't believe it. And I said hi back. I did. I'm a very forgiving person.

Mei tells me that three more of her family left Vietnam and have landed safely in Thailand. She tells me they should arrive any time and it's the first time I see her really smile. As much as I complain about my family, I couldn't imagine being forced to separate from them. She asks me to come for dinner the day after they are reunited, and I feel really honored that she wants me to share this happy time with them.

There is one person I'd really like to tell about what I'm doing. Andy. But he never did call me. A few weeks ago one of the Vietnamese asked me if I had a boyfriend. Of course I said no, but it got me thinking about him again. I'm tempted to write him, but I'm sure he has a girlfriend and he'd probably think I'm a pain. So really, only my family knows. They think it's great, I can tell you. My mom loves to see me off on Saturday mornings, knowing I'll be happy where I'm going. She grabbed my face in her hands last weekend and said, "It's so good to see you smile again!" She wants to cook a big dinner for all of my new friends. I'll invite them when the three others come.

I'm glad they will be arriving when it's nearly summer. I could tell this winter was pretty harsh for those refugees. They've come from pretty hot climates, and the city seems colder than the suburbs, with the wind howling between buildings. Luckily for them, their super heats their apartment almost to the point of unbearable, for me at least. I'm like my father; I love the cold. When I was in junior high, I used to call the weather number everyday in the winter when I got home from school and if it was above thirty, I'd get depressed. My dad would call from work and ask me how cold it was going to be. We'd both be pissed off if there was a warm front coming, but when those Canadian cold fronts would blow in, we'd be ecstatic! I still love the winter, but now I'm thinking about my refugee friends, and sixty and above feels better to them, so it's okay with me. In fact, I'm glad it's warm so I can take them to Ward Pound Ridge Reservation for a picnic. I think they'll like that.

Mei

Chapter 54

My heart is pounding as I sit in this van, as Danh drives us to John F. Kennedy International Airport. I clutch Linh's hand in my own. Tuan's face is bright with joy as he looks out at the New York City skyline. They are here! My sisters and brother have arrived and we are picking them up. They will see us when they disembark and walk through U.S. customs. They will not be alone!

Danh parks the van in the parking area and we four walk to the terminal. We have arrived early and check the board to see if their plane has arrived. It has, just. I am so nervous and excited, I hardly know how to sit and wait. Linh has made a sign with our family name on it which she taped to a ruler. She insists on standing near the gated area to hold it up. I tell her they will be quite some time, but she says she doesn't care, she will hold it up until they come out of the big doors. She is so proud of her sign. She is just learning to write her own name, yet she was resolute that she would hold up a sign for them, one she made herself. Holding the big fat marker in her tiny grip, she copied down the name I wrote for her on a piece of cardboard. The letters are large and uneven, but they are hers. She added little flowers and rainbows to decorate it.

I sit, I stand, I walk around. Tuan does the same. Danh smiles knowingly. He has done this many times. How many reunions has he witnessed, I wonder. I look at him when I see he is not looking at us and though I have met him on several occasions, I notice for the first time that he is very pleasant to look at. I wonder what his story is, but I am so shy, I have never yet asked. Mostly when I go to the office, it is Marion I speak to through various translators, but perhaps I might ask to speak to Danh, if I have the courage. I cannot believe I am thinking these thoughts when my sisters and brother are right through those gates. But then, perhaps it is because I feel happy. I am fatter now and much more pleasant to look at than when I first arrived. My hair is shiny and thick and the American shampoo smells wonderful. Why should I scold myself for these thoughts? Danh looks over at me, smiling, and I blush, but smile back at him. He looks down.

All of a sudden there is a commotion and I realize that people are streaming out of the gate. Mostly Chinese. This must be the flight we are waiting for! I stand next to Linh who is pressed up against the gate, holding her sign up for all to see. Tuan is behind a tall man and is jumping up and down to get a look at the people coming through. I hope I will recognize them. It has been almost a year since I have seen them. I pray they are healthy and not too skinny.

And then I see them! My sister Cam spots the sign and points and calls to Nhung, our other sister, my brother Hien following after! Linh, Tuan and I rush toward the gate's opening and grab our family out of the crowd and into our embrace. We are usually not so demonstrative, but we put aside custom, wrap our arms around our siblings, and hold tightly to them. I take in their flushed, drawn faces, their ragged clothes, their thin bodies, and I am determined to take good care of them so when we are reunited with our parents, they will know that I never wavered in my responsibility to my beloved family.

Danh takes the case from my second brother's hand and leads us in a merry march back to the van. I cannot stop touching them, their hair, their arms, patting their backs, grabbing their hands. Are they really here? My smile is broad, my relief immense.

My sisters and brother marvel at the sights as we cross the bridge on our drive back to the Bronx. Night is falling and the city sparkles like jewels. Cam and Nhung sit with me between them and snuggle into my shoulders. Hien sits between Tuan and Linh, who are holding his hands.

We are quiet until we return to our apartment, which I have cleaned until it sparkled. I invite Danh to come and eat with us, but he declines, saying that this is our time, perhaps another. I agree and thank him for all he has done today.

"I have only done my job," he replies, smiling.

"Then you have done a good job, because you have made us happy today. Thank you."

Tuan holds the battered case and we proudly show our siblings into their new home. There are three new beds on the floor, two in my room, one in Tuan's. They are made with new sheets and blankets, soft pillows. All the things I longed for and dreamed of. I can see that the three of them are exhausted and though I want to hear every detail of their experience, this must wait until they have rested.

"Is it really mine?" Cam asks quietly, pointing to the new bed the IRC brought to us.

"Of course it is yours. Would you like to lie down?" I know she would.

"Oh, yes, Number One Sister, very much. Is that all right?" she whispers. I nod and she tentatively sits down upon the mattress she has chosen for herself. I made sure the two new mattresses were far from the door, as is Linh's. I will be closest to the entrance. I will protect them. Cam smiles and places her head gently upon the pillow and Linh climbs onto the mattress next to her and snuggles tightly. They both close their eyes and I am sure Cam is asleep immediately.

Nhung has her arm through mine and we are just quiet. Tonight is not the time for chatter. Tomorrow, when they are refreshed, we will talk. I haven't told them about Hannah yet. I think they will find it a wonderful surprise.

I can hear my two brothers talking quietly in the next room. I wonder if anyone is hungry, but I think they are simply glad to be reunited with us. I will thank Kuan Yin tonight when I place my head upon my own pillow. I hope she won't find it presumptuous if I ask her to send more of my family. Perhaps I will thank her tonight and wait until tomorrow to ask for more favors. I want her to know my gratitude is immense.

Hannah

Chapter 55

School's out and Mei, Linh, Tuan, Hien, Cam, Nhung and I are on our way to Pound Ridge Reservation for a picnic. I feel kind of guilty not bringing the others, but I can barely fit all of them in my car as it is. I pack sandwiches, chips and fruit and they bring a case of 7-Up and tons of Vietnamese food in containers. I bring a Frisbee and a couple of balls. My sisters are not happy that they are not invited, but unless my father drives them here, there's no way we can all go.

It's a far drive from the Bronx, but I've been there tons of times and I can't think of a better place for a picnic. We tried to have a picnic at a park near their apartment, but when we set up our blanket on the scratchy balding grass, we heard tiny cries for help. Under a toppled garbage can were four newborn kittens. No mother in sight. So of course I insisted we take them and go back to the apartment. I took two home with me. I was going to take all four, but the kids wanted to keep two. Theirs died sooner than mine did, but not by much. I tried to feed them formula from a tiny bottle and they survived for a few days, but it didn't turn out well. The next time I went to the Bronx, the kids ran to me and told me their kittens had died.

So today, we'll go to Pound Ridge and hopefully not find any tiny, helpless, abandoned creatures. We'll just eat and play.

I am sure Mei praised me to the hilt, because the three newcomers, Hien, Nhung and Cam treat me like family. They looked so haggard and skinny the day I first met them. We had a big feast, just the Phoung family and me. I was so honored to be included in such a beautiful reunion meal.

The two girls are nine and eleven and I liked them immediately. Joni and Ruthie have met them a few times and they hit it off. It seems as if Hien has a crush on me. It is very sweet, his attentiveness, his constant staring. And he is cute and my age, but there's no way I can start anything with him. It would not be good. What if we broke up badly? I don't want anything to jeopardize my relationship with this family. Nope, it's not worth it. Anyway, I'm sure he only feels this way because I am always around.

They all came over for dinner a few weeks ago, after the three had settled in. My mother outdid herself cooking a wonderful dinner. We had spareribs, corn on the cob, baked beans and salad. Real American. She baked a carrot cake with cream cheese frosting for dessert and there was quite a discussion about using carrots in a sweet dessert. They seemed hesitant to try it, but you should have seen their faces when they ate it.

After dinner something strange happened. My mother has this huge coffee table book of art; Van Gogh, Monet, Renoir, that type of thing. I noticed Mei staring at it. Her hand reached out to it, but she didn't open it. It made me remember that time in Chinatown when she touched the window of that art supply store. I went over and sat down next to her on the couch and opened the book.

"This is beautiful, don't you think?" I asked, looking at Monet's water lilies.

"Oh, very beautiful. May I?" Mei asked me, as if wanting permission to turn the pages.

"Of course, Mei, that's what it's for. Are you interested in art?" I knew the answer now, but I wasn't sure if she was going to tell me.

"Yes. I love," she said, putting her eyes down. That's all she would say.

She was quiet and just staring at the pictures, turning the pages really slowly, as if savoring every page. I was going to ask her more questions, but Joni wanted to play cards with the younger ones and she wanted me there. I made a mental note to ask Mei about it soon. I have the feeling she has something brewing but I want to be careful. It may be painful to her.

I can feel Hien's eyes on me as I play Frisbee with Tuan and the girls.

"C'mon, Hien, play with us!" I call and wave. He comes over and I throw him the Frisbee, which he catches neatly. We play Frisbee and ball and drink tons of 7-Up until nearly eight. The days are longer again.

I've got to tell them that I'm going away for the whole month of August, back to Three Rivers. I hope they'll understand. Did they ever even hear of summer camp? The only camp they've probably heard of is a refugee camp. This makes me feel kind of guilty, but I'm going to be the Arts & Crafts counselor again this year and we'll be going ocean canoeing in Maine. I really want to go. And, of course, I'm pathetically hoping Andy will be back.

I'm not sure how to tell them, but I have to. I actually thought of canceling, but I love Three Rivers. And it's only for a month, not the whole summer.

Meí

Chapter 56

Hannah has told us she will be away for the entire month of August. I hate to say it, but we feel sick over this. We are spoiled by her attentions, I suppose. But the truth is, I feel safe and happy knowing she is a part of our lives, that she is connected with my family. Now that I am able to communicate with her more, I feel she is a dear friend. I know Hien will pine; he is so fond of her. Always moping when she leaves, brightening and moping at the same time when she is here. I tell him he must not like her that way. She is like our sister. She is particularly like an older sister to Linh, who will miss her most of all.

July was extremely hot, August hotter. It feels like Vietnam some days when the air is still with heat and the city seems to sweat. I relish this warmth though, knowing that winter will come again to this place. Our apartment is like a furnace and the windows are difficult to open. They seem to have swelled and are stuck shut. Even my strong brothers cannot open them. I bought a small fan, but it only circulates the steam.

My sisters look longingly at the fire hydrants that spray water where many neighborhood children cool themselves, but they have not been to school yet and therefore have almost no English, so are too afraid to try to make friends. And then, out of the blue, Hannah's mother calls and invites us to come over. Hannah's father will pick us up. Tuan speaks to her and makes the arrangements. I shake my head, marveling at this family, who would extend their friendship to people so foreign to them. My sisters are bursting when I tell them the news.

"Will Hannah be there?"

"No, she is away, but her sisters will play with you!"

They are excited but my anxiety is high. What will I say to Hannah's parents? Although I am learning, I am ashamed of my inability to express myself in English.

"I cannot go, I must work," Hien tells me.

"All right, then, you work. Work is good and we need the money. Tuan?"

"Of course I will go."

And so, Hannah's father picks us up in his station wagon and carries us to their home. Hannah's mother and sisters are waiting outside when we arrive and there is a good smell of barbecuing meat. They have a small garden with a metal swing set and soon the girls are all playing together happily. There is a table set with a red checkered cloth and bowls of vegetables and chips which I see Hannah's parents dipping into creamy white sauce. Tuan and I shyly take what is offered, dipping our carrot or potato chip into what is called "dip" and finding that we like it.

"This is French onion dip. It's my favorite," Hannah's mother says, smiling.

"I like," I say, not fully understanding but trying to make conversation.

"When Hannah return?" Tuan asks.

"In another two weeks or so...." She continues speaking but I am lost. I must look strange because Hannah's mother claps her hand over her mouth and turns red. "I'm so sorry! I was speaking much too quickly. Did you understand what I said?" This she says very slowly so I can understand.

"Little," I reply, embarrassed. Not one word.

"I understand," Tuan says.

"Hannah is canoeing... a canoe is a boat with paddles, like this," she demonstrates. I nod. "She's canoeing in the ocean and she will be home in two weeks."

"Mom, when's dinner?" Hannah's sister, Joni, yells. I am grateful.

"Is everybody hungry?" Hannah father has a booming voice, but I am not frightened. He has a kind smile as he stands over the hot coals and turns over the meat. We all nod our heads, hoping this is the right thing to do. Without Hannah here to guide us, it is hard to know. I think we are doing all right, though.

"Hamburgers! Very American," Hannah's father says proudly. We copy Joni and Ruthie as they put their circle of grilled meat on bread and cover it in red sauce. I take a bite. It is delicious.

I am relieved because the conversation now turns to things like, "Do you like this?" and "Mmn, this is very good..." and "Do they have this in Vietnam?" I promise myself to study English more diligently.

After dinner, Hannah's father drives us home. I am embarrassed for his trouble, but I would never let him know this. I wish we could have taken a bus to save him from this inconvenience, but I know he would never permit it. My sisters sit far in the back with Hannah's sisters who accompany their father on this drive. They chat with one another, though I have no idea how they communicate. I am quiet, wondering what Hannah's father thinks about us. He plays the radio loudly, Western classical music, which I find comforting. I can tell he is a cultured man.

I secretly wish I could have looked once more at the book of art in Hannah's living room. My hand has been still for so long, I wonder if I will remember how to carefully stroke the paper with a brush. I have been secretly saving a few pennies every payday so that I can return to the art shop I saw when we went to Chinatown. The stirrings of a painting are beginning to awaken within me.

We stand on the street together shaking hands and saying goodbye.

"Thank you, sir," we all say to Hannah's father.

"You are very welcome," he says in his booming voice. "Hannah will call you as soon as she gets back!"

The girls are waving to each other and we continue to stand there until they drive away. I wonder if any other refugees are as fortunate as we. My three young sisters are holding hands as they skip down the walk to our apartment.

I smile at Tuan who grins back at me.

Hannah

Chapter 57

I love the Project! Oh, my God, it's incredible and if I thought for one minute about how school could have been the last three years if I had been here, I might have to weep from regret! I've already made a couple of friends! Even I can hardly believe it. My Jewish mother practically genuflects every time she drives by the church where this school is housed.

My schedule is as follows: Morning meeting, which is this amazing time where we talk about the day ahead, dreams we've had, any cool experiences we'd like to share. And I do! I share! I actually share! My heart pounds, but I do it anyway, and no one makes fun of me! Everybody listens. I tell about my experience ocean canoeing off the coast of Maine, and how we camped on the beach and cooked lobster in pits covered with seaweed. And how ocean canoeing is completely different from canoeing on lakes. People ask questions, and I answer, not embarrassed at all. And other people share too, and everyone is sincerely interested!

After morning meeting is Social Studies with the coolest teacher. There are only seven other students in the class and we talk about what we read the previous night. We are working on the Civil War and Reconstruction. The teacher speaks from experience about stories his grandmother told him about her own grandparents, who actually were slaves!

Then we get into this discussion about civil rights and the Vietnam War. I am so tempted to talk about my work with the refugees, but it feels like it might be showing off so I keep quiet. For now.

After that is English, where the teacher wants loads of creative writing from us. And that I can do!

Then there's art. We've been doing pen and ink drawings and the teacher asked me to submit some of mine to the yearbook! I really cannot believe this. At the high school, I felt like I was number 254 or whatever, but here, I'm Hannah and people are starting to know me, and I'm letting them.

Science is near the end of the day and we spend it outdoors, observing and collecting from a stream nearby, testing the water for pollutants.

My last class is photography. It's my favorite class and it is here that I first develop my pictures of the refugees. I have a few undeveloped rolls of black and white that I've been saving for some reason. For the first couple of months I worked with the families, I didn't dare bring my Pentax, but after a while, I started taking it with me and very discreetly started taking pictures, with permission of course. I had the color pictures developed at the camera shop and brought them to share, but these black and whites, I don't know. I suppose I could have developed them at the high school dark room, but I didn't really want to share them with anyone there. Here at the Project, I know no one will think I'm a geek 'cause I spend all my weekends helping refugees, rather than partying. And as I place the paper in the fixer and see little Linh's face appear out of the darkness, I am rather impressed with myself. And my teacher is, too. He wants to know who she is and what's the story behind the sad eyes. And I tell him. And it feels great to share it. Finally. He wants to display these in the halls at school. He says I should be really proud of myself. Not just for the quality of the pictures, but for what I'm doing. I hadn't really thought about it that way, but I guess I am proud of myself.

I'm especially thrilled about what I did right after I got back from Three Rivers. I'd been thinking a lot about that day in Chinatown, when Mei put her hand on that art store window. And also the day at my house where she looked through my mom's art book as though it was a precious thing. I had the feeling she had stuff brewing inside, but I didn't want to pry. Instead, I brought her paints and brushes from Three Rivers. I didn't steal them or anything, but since I was the arts and crafts counselor, when we were cleaning up at the end of camp, the director asked me if I wanted anything. The paints wouldn't keep for a whole year in an unheated cabin, so I said yes and took all the leftover watercolors and tempera paints, a couple of old brushes and some paper.

My hunch was right. I wrapped them in tissue paper, like a gift, and gave them to Mei. At first I thought I did something wrong because she began to cry. Just softly, but I felt my cheeks burn thinking maybe I'd brought back memories that were too painful for her to take. But that wasn't it. She looked at me through her tears and smiled this smile of gratitude. I just smiled back. There was nothing to say. I didn't ask her to paint anything right then and there, but she got up, wiped her eyes and went into the kitchen to get a bowl of water. And she started to paint.

What came from her hand, out of those paints and onto that paper was amazing. Amazing. And she gave that first one to me.

Mei

Chapter 58

My hand is no longer still. My mind no longer filled with anguish that has no escape. Instead, images are flowing from mind to hand to paper where they now live. I am painting again and it feels like I was unconscious and have awakened. Like I was a prisoner who has been set free.

I think Hannah might be a mind reader. One of those rare people who know and understand what lies hidden deep within a person. I thought I had kept my secret hidden from everyone. My longing. I thought I had conquered my need to lift brush to paper. That I had become responsible, that painting was only a frivolity that I should do without. But Hannah knew. Like she knew we needed her, she knew I needed to paint and she brought me paints.

"This is for you, Mei," Hannah said, handing me a wrapped package when she came to see us after her summer job was done.

"What is this, Hannah? There is no need to bring me gifts."

"Oh, yes there is, Mei. Open it!"

"Yes, yes, First Sister, open the gift!" my brothers and sisters called.

They watched as I gently lifted the tape off the brightly colored package, carefully unfolding the lovely paper. They saw my face change as I realized what was in the box. Linh clapped her hands in delight and said in English, "Sister makes pretty pictures, Hannah, you see!"

I can say that I am not ashamed of how I behaved when she presented me with this gift. I do not blush at the thought. I am not mortified. I simply cried. Nothing more. It started as a gasp at first, from deep within my core. An agonizing pain that was suddenly released. And then finally, my tears were able to lift from my heart into my eyes and flow.

I know Hannah was worried by my moan, but I smiled in gratitude and I know she understood. And then I did something I have never done before. First I went into the kitchen and filled a bowl with water. I returned and laid out the paper on the table and spread the colors in front of me. Everyone was staring, their eyes wide. Never before had I practiced my art in front of anyone except my teacher. Painting for me had always been a very private activity. But this day, I needed to share it.

They were very quiet as I took the big black brush that had come in the package and dipped it into the water. I chose a color and let the water from the brush soften its hardness, and then holding the brush as I was taught, I slowly and deliberately allowed it to ever so gently stroke the paper. Green leaves, buds, a flower - simple. Rebirth. I looked at what I had done and felt a warmth spread through me like a small fire. From nothing I created beauty. When I was done I found the smallest brush in the package, wet it, dipped it into black paint and wrote my Chinese name. As I always did. Do. I handed the painting to Hannah.

"For you, my dear friend," I said, in perfect English.

Hannah whispered back to me, her voice choked with emotion, "Thank you, dear friend."

My colors are vibrant, my images strong. I paint alone, I paint in company. I paint on rice paper, I paint on silk. I paint landscapes, I paint faces. My paintings sustain me and keep me whole. They are the past, the present, the future. They are me. Mei.

Epilogue

This story is a fictionalized account based on true events. Thirty years later, Hannah and Mei's family continue to be wonderful friends. Hannah was there for every reunion. In fact, she was the one chosen to meet Mei's parents at the airport when they finally arrived in the U.S. some 3 years later. When Hannah got married, Mei was there. And Hannah was there for many weddings and births.

Hannah went on to college, majoring in Chinese studies and anthropology. She eventually got a job at the International Rescue Committee (IRC) where she worked as a caseworker (like Marion) with families from Vietnam, Cambodia, and Laos until 1986 when President Reagan slashed the non-profit budget and she and many others lost their jobs. She continues to work with immigrants and refugees today.

The five families that Hannah worked with are all very successful. Many own stores in New York's Chinatown; all the children continued their education and have gone on to become architects, teachers, chiropractors and accountants. They live in many parts of the United States. Some have returned to Vietnam for a visit.

Mei still paints. And Mei and Hannah are still dear friends.

For information on how you can volunteer, there are many exciting websites that have a wide variety of volunteering opportunities.

Go to **www.theirc.org** or **www.volunteers.com** today!

Acknowledgments

I would like to acknowledge the many people who helped me with the creation and completion of this book. Linda, thank you for your understanding of what I was trying to accomplish and especially for your invaluable knowledge and input. Thanks to the Q. family for the call about the carrot cake. It was my springboard!

To Joe, Sam and Zoë, for listening to me go on endlessly about this story and for putting up with the many take-out (so I can write) meals, I love you so much! Again to Zoë, my best reader, editor and biggest fan - I'm *your* biggest fan!

Thanks to my amazing friend Belle, who has helped with this project in more ways than I can say. You are a genius! Thanks to Ariana for your constant guidance in helping me see this project realized and keeping me pointed downstream. To my kind readers: Marion, Diane, Dahlia, Danielle, Maddy, Tara, Sheena, WindRose, Mari, Shirley, Rachel, Brianna, Lina, Pauline, and Emmanuel - your constructive comments and enthusiasm gave me the courage to let this story out into the world. Thanks to my cheerleaders - Mama Rose, Gina, Angel, Anderson, Maeve, Heidi, Cathy, Laura, Ikumi, Nefertiti, Nathan, Peggy, Ann, Theresa, Debbie, Di & my entire far-flung family!

To my beautiful sisters, Pamela and Toni who continue to encourage me and who were an integral part of this story, I love you guys. Dad, thank you for your constant support and faith in me. And thanks to my mom, who allowed me to read to her over and over again, and who laughed and cried with me in all the right places during the entire birthing process and never once stopped believing in me.

I am blessed to have you all in my life.

Jana Laiz, Winter 2008

Coming Soon!

The Twelfth Stone

By Jana Laiz

I met a lady in the meads
Full beautiful - a faery's child;
Her hair was long, her foot was light,
And her eyes were wild.

John Keats, La Belle Dame Sans Merci, IV

Chapter 1

"I willna marry him. Ye canna force me!" Rionnag spoke defiantly, with more courage than she actually felt.

"Och, aye, I can and I will and there's naught ye'll do about it!" her mother said.

"Then I'll go before ye put yer marriage shackles around my neck!"

"Ye'll go right tae the altar, that's what! Ye will no disgrace us or yerself!" When her mother spoke like this she knew there would be no argument.

Rionnag tossed her head back and went to her room. Let her mother think she'd won. She would wait for night and the moon and then she'd leave. Her parents had arranged this marriage when she was a wee bairn, but according to custom, she couldn't meet him until the wedding day. How unfair! she thought.

"Mòr, please brush my hair," she entreated her maid whom she knew hovered outside the door. It always made her feel better to have her long hair stroked. The door, which had been ajar, was flung open and Mòr entered unceremoniously, Ceitidh, Mòr's aide, following in her wake.

"Certainly. If ye wouldna be sae defiant, yer mither wouldna be in such a state all the time." The maid, who had been in charge of her since the day she was born had no qualms about speaking her mind to the girl.

"Weel, do ye no think my situation is intolerable?" Rionnag demanded.

"Aye, that I do, but that has naught to do wi' it. I ken what yer feeling, but yer mither willna bend in this matter to be sure." The maid removed the foxglove cap from Rionnag's fair head and began brushing her silken hair.

"Weel, she'll soon see that I am not sae easily forced," she replied with a gesture indicating the conversation was at an end.

Mòr on the other hand was not so eager to end it. "Listen to me, my girl, I love ye as if ye were my own bairn..."

"I wish I was," Rionnag interrupted

"Let me finish. Ye are the daughter of a queen and king and in matters of marriage, it is yer duty to obey yer parents. I ken ye don't love the lad, but in time ye may..."

"Love him! Mòr, I've never even met him. Ye ken that!"

"Princess, speak like a lady!"

She rolled her eyes, "Yes, right. Ye know that I do not love him!"

"Aye, that I do, but I hear tell he's a fine lad. Handsome too!" she winked at the girl trying to lighten the situation.

“Aye, I’ve heard Prince Kier… Ooh, ah, the prince is a lovely boy…” Ceitidh blundered, blushing scarlet. Even the prince’s name was not to be spoken in front of his bride. Poor Ceitidh rarely said anything lest Mòr scold her, and though Mòr said nothing, she gave her subordinate a withering glance.

“I dinna care for looks. That’s no the point of the matter. What of my choice? Nay, I willna go through wi’ it,” she declared and she threw herself down on the bed. Mòr sat down beside her, her bulk nearly tilting the bed over, and patted the hair of her lass.

Rionnag's statement was true. She cared nothing for looks, and Mòr knew this because for all the lass’ beauty, she hadn't a vain bone in her body. Rionnag was the bonniest of all the lassies in the hill, the envy of many. Her hair shone golden and curled naturally at the bottom, her eyes were the darkest violet with an amethyst cast to them. They shone as if there were tears welling just below the surface, but Rionnag's sure smile indicated that if there were any tears, they were tears of laughter. That smile formed on a full mouth was the object of many a lad's fancy.

Mòr stayed until she thought the girl was asleep and quietly left the room. As soon as the maid was gone, Rionnag opened her eyes and looked around her chamber. The gnarled wooden bed with its webbed canopy and blanket of spun silk was the place she liked best to dream. Sweet peas, violets, and periwinkles grew in profusion on their covering of soft green, perfuming the air. Her birch chair in the corner was where she spent many the hour curled up with a book. She would miss this place, but her mind was made up. When the moon rose, she would leave.

There was a knock on the door and in walked a handsome man wearing a robe of the finest velvet. His hair was ebony, his eyes indigo. Upon his head he wore a crown of gold, encrusted with blue stones that matched his eyes: Tanzanite stones, for power. The antlers, normally prominent, at the moment were retracted until only the tips showed from within the circle of the crown. He looked fiercely at the girl, but then his look softened to one of fatherly love.

"Why do ye give yer mither such trouble, my lassie?" her father asked.

"Oh, Faither, I dinna want to marry. I want to stay here and be with ye! Why must ye force me to do this thing?" She nearly cried out the words.

"Rionnag Ban, my daughter, this is a matter of the Seelie Court. Ye are a princess of that Court, and ye must abide by its rules. Ye know that! This marriage has been planned since ye were wee and if ye don't go through wi' it, there'll be trouble from the court."

"I dinna care what the court does!"

"Child, ye must remember, it isna only the court that will be affected if ye don't wed. All of Faerie will feel it." He hesitated before he went on, weighing his words carefully. He looked at his wild-eyed daughter, the blessing of his life, and yearned for her to be a bairn again. But this, the year she was to be wed was upon them and this marriage was ordained.

"Ye'll no be far from here when ye wed. I'll see to it. But Rionnag, ye have been told the truth of what is happening to our world. The dark forces are gathering as the old forests are destroyed, as the earth is befouled. Come, look." He took her by the hand and led her to her window. She could see the encroaching gloom, the dark shadowy tendrils creeping around bush and briar. She turned her head away, but her father gently turned it back, forcing her to take another look at what was happening, even within the royal lands. She pulled away once more, pushing aside all thoughts but how unfair this marriage seemed. Her father took her face in his hands.

“Lassie, I’m that sorry to say, Faerie is fading. Yer marriage with the Prince of Ireland’s Daoine Sidhe will strengthen the pure side, and perhaps save our way of life. I know it is a great responsibility, overwhelming perhaps, but do not fret, I’ll still be King for some time, and yer mither will still be Queen. So please, don’t rile us again. Next time I willna be sae understanding.” With that he kissed his daughter on the top of her head and left the chamber.

“Acchh!” she spat out. She had barely heard a word he said, her ire was so high. How could her loving father not budge? Why must she be of royal blood? Who cared what the Seelie Court did? Her resolve became stronger as she waited for the rising of the moon.

From her bed she looked out and listened to the familiar sounds of twilight. The birds were chattering their goodnights to one another. She saw the outline of an owl fly past, early, she thought, and heard the muffled scream as he took his first victim. Finally, after what seemed like hours, the moon peered from behind the great Rowan tree outside her window and spread dappled light throughout the forest. She took a last look around her room, and opening her iridescent wings, lifted herself out of the window. She landed high on the branch of the familiar Rowan and crouched for a few moments to listen. Tonight, there were no other sounds. No music, no bells, nor pipes, nor fiddles. No songs, nor voices carried on the soft breeze. How fortuitous.

Her heart tripped erratically in her chest as she left the branch and headed for the old ring. Remembering the ominous shadows, she looked behind her nervously as she made her way to her destination. She had found it only days before, nearly hidden among the overgrown brush. The old stones were tumbled and worn, standing in their circle of power. She could tell that it was a rarely used ring from the distant past, but one that none would think to look for and her essence would be long gone by the time they might discover it. She had only gone through a ring once with her father, a long time ago, when she was a wee thing, but that was a popular ring that was used every feast night. Her father had wanted to show her the other side, its beauties and dangers. It had been Samhain then and easy to get across, unlike this night, which was no feast night. She had never forgotten the colors and the way the light fell there and it seemed the perfect place to go to escape what she perceived as such a cruel fate.

She followed the path from Rowan to Oak to Birch to Ash until she found the spot. She looked around to make sure no one was watching. A hedgehog gawked at her then hurried away. A Pixie spy? No, just a hedgehog, she told herself. She found the ring just as she had left it. No one had disturbed it. The stones in their circle of power were worn with age. Moss and fallen leaves covered them, the fey symbols made illegible by time. She circled above it several times trying to give herself the resolve to follow through with her plan. She had no idea where she would come through on the other side, but it had to be better than a forced marriage. She took a deep breath and muttered the old words to herself. She had learned the words from her mother's lexicon of spells, an ancient volume containing various magics, from mixing up hurricanes, to capturing changelings and mortals, to crossing over to the other side. Rionnag had found the book when her mother was busy with the Council, so involved with the rapidly shifting and precarious conditions of the seasons, she scarce remembered she had a daughter.

She'd had to memorize the words quickly. Her mother would have been in a rare state had she found Rionnag with the book. Only those adept in wielding power were entitled to use that book, and Rionnag was neither ready nor skilled enough. Now, as she eyed the ring, she prayed she would remember.

The words were old, older even than the ancient tongue she spoke. She had to practice them until they were strong in her mind. Any mistake could prove dangerous, even fatal. She took a last look around. Then, collecting her courage, she made the old symbol, recited the spell, and stepped through the ring.

JANA LAIZ has been writing for as long as she can remember. In addition to writing the Award Winning novel, *Weeping Under This Same Moon*, she is the author of *Elephants of the Tsunami*, and the co-author of *"A Free Woman On God's Earth"*, The True Story of Elizabeth "Mumbet" Freeman, The Slave Who Won Her Freedom. Fascinated by other cultures, Jana studied anthropology and Chinese language at University. She is a teacher, a writer, an editor, a publisher, a photographer, a mom, an animal lover and keeper of pets, a sea glass collector, a jeweler, a musician and a dreamer. Jana was a caseworker at The International Rescue Committee working in refugee resettlement. She is passionate about our beautiful planet and endeavors to make a difference in the world and to work with others who feel the same. She lives in The Berkshires, Massachusetts. Visit her at www.janalaiz.com

Photo by Jane Feldman